THE HERO OF FERN GULLY

AND OTHER JAMAICAN SHORT STORIES

BASIL KONG
GLEN LAMAN

ISBN: 978-1-7353069-4-0 (Softcover)

Editor: Lena Joy Rose

Layout and Design: Mark Weinberger

Printed in United States of America

Ordering Information:
Quantity (Bulk) Sales. Special discounts are available on
quantity (bulk) purchases by corporations, associations, and
others. For details, contact the authors:
bwaine@zoepeds.com
glenlaman@gmail.com

Other Books

Bad Boy from Jamaica: The Garnett Myrie Story

Basil Kong

ISBN 978-149-90104-1-1 (Paperback)

Jamaican Entrepreneurship

Glen Laman

ISBN 978-976-95693-1-7 (Paperback)

ISBN 978-057-84422-7-3 (e-Book)

Contents

Dedication

We dedicate this book to all those who
played a part in our Jamaican upbringing:
the teachers, ministers, shopkeepers, grandparents,
parents, uncles, aunts, siblings, cousins, relatives,
boyhood friends and neighbors.

Foreword

Jamaica is an island known for friendly and hospitable people, rum, reggae, beautiful white sand beaches, and radiant sunshine. Numerous luminaries have made an impact on the world stage. These include Bob Marley, Toots and the Maytals, Grace Jones, Shelly Ann Fraser Pryce, Mary Seacole and Usain Bolt, but still left to be told are the enchanting vault of stories around the life of the ordinary Jamaican man, woman, and child.

Basil Kong and Glen Laman have written 15 charming stories that capture the essence of several typical Jamaican situations in their memorable book, *The Hero of Fern Gully and Other Jamaican Short Stories.*

The book delivers a fascinating glimpse of another side of Jamaican island life. You will be transported to historic Fern Gully, in the parish of St. Ann, and the leafy, meandering hills that shoulder Lovers Leap in Southfield, St. Elizabeth. You will celebrate Christmas in the rustic countryside of Woodside: feel Mattie's struggles in her quest to build her dream home, be drawn to the treats, the delights of Miss Bailey's Cold Supper Shop, and see tourists through the eyes of an innkeeper.

Adults and teens will enjoy reading this treasure trove of stories celebrating ordinary happenings around ordinary people with an extraordinary legacy.

I am highly recommending this great read where you will discover, or rediscover, what life is like where the "sun shines daily on the mountain top" and "the ackee, rice n' saltfish nice so till" as these island people pursue "one love" and try to "feel alright."

Pull up *yu* chair, cock up *yu* foot and make space to experience precious, simple, but very colourful memories.

—— Debra Ehrhardt

Debra Ehrhardt is an award-winning actress and playwright. She is best known for the highly acclaimed play and soon to be motion picture, Jamaica Farewell

Preface

The authors, Basil Kong and Glen Laman, are like 'brothers.' They have each been mistaken for the other. They resemble each other and are close in age, height, weight, hairstyle, and complexion.

Both grew up poor in rural Jamaica—*aka* "country." Glen grew up in the parish of St. Ann while Basil grew up in St. Elizabeth and both migrated to the United States as teenagers.

They first met when Glen worked at the Coca-Cola Company in Atlanta, Georgia, as a project manager and Basil was the CEO of the Association of Black Cardiologists. When Basil first saw Glen, he thought he was looking in the mirror and was compelled to introduce himself. Glen immediately said, "So, you are the guy who has caused me to be accused of so many crimes and indiscretions!" They quickly became fast friends and as they recounted memorable childhood incidents, they uncovered an enduring passion for their island in the sun. Jamaica was always on their minds.

When the pandemic of 2020 restricted social interaction and everyone looked for activities to help maintain their sanity, they decided that a book of Jamaican short stories would be a worthy project. It would also be a way to keep their memories alive, especially for all who will come after them. They were both published authors as Basil had written *Bad Boy from Jamaica: The Garnett Myrie Story,* while Glen had penned *Jamaican Entrepreneurship* several years prior.

The 15 stories in **The Hero of Fern Gully and Other Jamaican Short Stories** provide insights into the everyday pursuits of ordinary Jamaicans as they struggle to make a way in this world. Some satories may make you laugh, and others may bring a tear. Readers who grew up in the 1950s and 1960s can also relate to a bygone era when life was simpler, and people were poor but dignified. Despite many hardships, Jamaicans are a happy and hospitable people. In the end, we hope you will come away with a better appreciation and understanding of the Jamaican spirit.

AUTHOR'S NOTE

Rosie's story is so real. It reminds us of the derivation of Jamaica's motto, "Out of Many One People." However, as her story shows it is not always an easy road to live up to this motto. And while many advances have been made in terms of race and class on the island, a look back in time reveals the stark reality of another era. It is a story of the power of love to overcome family and societal obstacles.

Nobody Knows the Trouble I've Seen—Rosie's Story

Basil Kong

How did my brother and I come to live with our grandmother Rosie?

In 1947, my father abandoned our family and returned home to China. I was just four years old and my brother Earl was three. Out of desperation, my mother decided to accept her sister Elaine's invitation to migrate to the United States. Elaine had previously settled in the United States with her husband and two daughters.

Suddenly, in the middle of the night, my mother loaded a truck with a spring bed, a bureau and other pieces of furniture and took us from Kingston to Woodside, St. Elizabeth. She left her children in the care of her mother and returned to Kingston to depart for the United States the next day.

My brother and I thrived in our grandmother's care. We were poor and had to contend with an outdoor toilet, wood fires, no electricity, and no running water, but she provided plenty of good food and loving kindness. I am sure we had more hugs and kisses growing up than any other kids on the planet.

As soon as the rooster crowed at dawn each morning, Granny would roll out of bed and start her day down on her knees with prayer. In fact, my brother and I would wake up to her singing a hymn of praise.

I remember when I was about twelve years old, she would get up after praying and singing:

"Nobody knows the trouble I have seen; nobody knows but Jesus. Nobody knows my sorrow."

I wondered what she meant so I asked her, "what trouble have you seen Granny?"

"Well son, I will tell you the whole story if you help Granny with a few chores."

For the rest of the day, I followed her around and helped her with whatever she was doing while listening to her stories. We made all the beds, washed, and hung clothes out to dry, cooked banana porridge, slopped the pigs, picked a breadfruit, and even killed a chicken for dinner. I never realized how much work my poor old Granny did. She never seemed tired and even had time for brewing coffee that she shared with neighbors who predictably stopped by.

Granny told me she was born in 1888 to William McNab and Maria Carter. Both her parents took the names of their slave masters and so that is how she ended up being a McNab.

When the English abolished slavery in their colonies on August 1, 1834, the Crown (English Parliament) paid slave owners in full for their slaves—purchased for a price so they could be set free—but unfortunately, there was no money for the slaves who had endured two hundred years of brutal servitude.

Slave-owners who profited from free labor were further enriched by these government grants that did nothing for the slaves themselves. As soon as the slaves were freed, many ran away fearing that they would be caught again and put back in chains. Many would end up in the most inhospitable places with land that would never appreciate in value. Slave owners and their families continued to own big houses, factories, plantations, and beachfront properties. With the funds from Queen Victoria, most of the wealthy plantation owners returned to England leaving behind their poor cousins who would continue to enjoy White privilege.

The customs of the slave system persisted with white people enjoying economic advantages and respect. As there were over one hundred applicants for every available job, former slaves had to compete aggressively with each other and had to accept whatever was offered. Often, those salaries were just one step above slave labor. Other than subsistence farming on small plots of land, their individual survival was almost entirely dependent on the good will of the White people. Pissing off one of them was tantamount to making enemies of all of them and to risk starvation.

Granny went on to tell me that when she was fifteen years old, all the boys were very interested in her.

"You can't really tell now, but your Granny was quite a looker and was kept very busy making excuses to keep them away as my father would have killed me," she explained.

She said she took a fancy to this older white boy named Will Robinson and he took a powerful liking to her as well. You should have seen the twinkle in her eye when she told me that they were deeply in love and found each other irresistible. I was so mesmerized with her story that I almost tripped when going down some steps.

Granny said they were in love and irresistible lovers. There was a broad smile on his face whenever he saw her. He was always writing her love poems and slipping them in her apron pocket. They would see each other every day but his mother hated her and told him that a Black woman would never be allowed in her house.

When they talked about getting married, Will said that could never happen because his mother wouldn't allow it. So, she cussed out both him and his mama and started seeing another boy, Cleve Shaw, who was always telling her how much he loved her. He had a house and he asked her to marry him and so Granny moved in with him. This story was better than a movie.

She went on to say that she heard through the grapevine that Will was having a hard time getting over her. He couldn't eat, sleep, was inconsolable and stayed in his bed all the time. Served him right!

"Me hear say that him tell his Pupa that he couldn't live without me. But I was done with the whole of them people," she told me as she bussed out a big laugh.

Will's father was sympathetic and had helped him build a house on a piece of family land. After six months, Will, Granny's old boyfriend, marches into their yard and walks straight up to Cleve. He tells him that Granny is his woman and that he has come for her.

"No, you're not. Move outa me yard. She is mine now," says Cleve defiantly.

Hot tempered Will punched Cleve and they get into a rass fight. Finally, Cleve gives up.

"All right, take her, it's you she love anyway."

Will picked Granny up, put her on his shoulders and carries her to his house. She was kicking and protesting all the way.

"Put me down you piece of cow dung. I don't want to have anything to do with your stupid family."

"You are my woman, and this is your house."

"So," Granny asked him, "What took you so long. I was waiting for you."

And as soon as she said that he grabbed her and he couldn't stop loving her up for the rest of the day and night. Will's father was happy for them, but his mother still didn't accept her.

The surprise was that Granny was pregnant with Cleve's baby. Will was not happy.

"Damn it Rosie, did you have to do that to me?"

"You blaming me? No sah, me is not the one to blame. Blame your stupid mother. She knew we loved each other."

So, their first child, a daughter, was black and was not the apple of Will's eye. As much as Rosie defended her first born, Will could never bring himself to treat her like his own or send her to school. As soon as she was fourteen years old, she was sent away to Kingston, a bitter and some say a hateful young woman.

Still, Will and Granny could not keep away from each other. Even when they worked in the garden they were like rabbits whenever she lifted her dress to show him her legs.

In 20 years they had 14 children.

Some were white, some black and every shade in between.

In between having so many children, they worked hard on the piece of land his father allowed them to farm and raise cows, hogs, and chickens. In 1933, they brought in a crop of corn and loaded up their living room and invited friends to come over for an all-night shelling party. Their intention was to bag the corn and take it to market. That night Granny thought Will had fallen asleep but when she tried to rouse him, she discovered he was dead from a heart attack. His father had also died early of a heart attack.

Tears welled up in her eyes as she continued with her story.

"If my screams and tears could have brought him back, he would have been alive today." He was fifty and our youngest son was only four years old.

Compounding the problem of feeding so many children, Granny was not married to Will. His mother ordered everyone to get off her property thereby making Granny and her own grandchildren homeless. I was in complete shock with my mouth wide open. How cruel was that?

Granny looked at me and remarked, "Now, do you understand the trouble I have seen?"

So, when I finally closed my mouth, I asked Granny what happened after that.

She said that in about a month she was able to borrow some money to buy a piece of land. She dismantled the house that Will built and resurrected it by the roadside—nothing fancy, just three rooms where the children had to sleep head to foot. Her daughter and my mother helped her to add one more room after Earl and I came to live with her.

As God would have it, the older children were able to send help. Her oldest son John joined the police force, married and settled down in Mile Gully, Manchester. Her first born Myrtle married Mr. Brown, a veteran returning from World War 11 who worked at Victoria Jubilee Hospital. He had also learned how to extract teeth in the Army and made money on the side as a dentist even though he never went to dental school. My mother and Sylvia went to live with them.

According to Granny, when my mother was going around Kingston looking for work, she made inquiries at my father's restaurant, Kong's Ice Cream Parlor on Water Street. He immediately hired her as a cashier. I was born a year later, and my brother Earl was born a year after that. My father had bought mother a house.

Her daughter Edna was welcomed into the household of the rich Miles family in Santa Cruz where Lenny was five years older than her. She didn't like it but, at fifteen years old, they became lovers with the support and approval of his parents.

When Lenny became sick with a virus and they believed that he would not survive, my mother reminded them that if they did not get married and he died, the Miles family would treat Edna just like Will's mother had treated Granny and kick her out of their house with no means of support, so Violet obtained the services of a Minister and they were married at the hospital. Lenny survived and they had three more children.

Two of Granny's children died at birth and two died of natural causes. Randall died in his teens of some mysterious disease and Kendall was run over by a bull. I ended up with an amazing family who are now all doing well.

"Through it all, I learned to depend upon the Lord. I am telling you all this to let you know that God will provide and as much tribulations you may encounter in your life, he will take care of you. Just trust and obey."

My mother made a new life in America. She married an American and started a new family. They would later greet us when my brother and I joined them in Morristown, New Jersey in 1959. I was fifteen years old. Until then, I would not have been able to pick out either my mother or father in a police line-up; I could not have recognized either one of them.

I have never seen my father since he left us.

In every seed, there is the promise of a forest. Ms. Rosie's offspring now number over 100 mostly residing in the United States. Among them are several educated and prosperous descendants. According to Granny, if you plant seeds of kindness, you will reap a bountiful harvest.

AUTHOR'S NOTE

Jamaicans are naturally entrepreneurial. They are out of necessity always "trying-a-ting" to improve their life. They pursue this path usually because they lack the education to get a job or because there are not enough jobs available.

Miss Bailey, in "Miss Bailey's Cold Supper Shop," embodies that spirit. Such shops were plentiful in the inner city of Kingston in an era before refrigeration. The menus were also limited and catered primarily to single working men.

People of Miss Bailey's generation, who grew up under colonialism, had limited access to a secondary education. This all changed with the drive for independence as the government began offering a number of free places to high schools once reserved for the privileged.

Miss Bailey's Cold Supper Shop

Glen Laman

I walk down the stairs and head toward the gate, maneuvering under a clothesline full of bras and panties hanging out to dry across the yard. Several small dogs start barking. Two women washing clothes by the standpipe and cistern near the center of the yard look up and yell at the dogs to hush.

Once on the street, I head north on Rum Lane turning left onto Rosemary Lane. I cross the busy East Queen Street carefully as the traffic moves quickly on this busy thoroughfare. It is a Saturday morning and folks are busy going to market and catching up on errands they have to run.

I cross Beeston Street and Charles Street before arriving at Miss Bailey's "cold supper" shop on the right. These tiny, hole-in-the-wall shops are scattered across the inner city. These struggling enterprises are usually hanging by a thread financially. They serve a few cooked food items, usually cold, for take-out.

Miss Bailey's is not your run-of-the-mill cold supper shop, however. It is a thriving small business. The spicy aroma of oxtail, with broad beans, and escoveitch fish, with vinegar, greets me at the door.

"Yes, sir. What can I help you with?" says the woman behind the counter.

"Me come to see Miss Bailey. Tell her it's Stephen."

"Miss Bailey, she hollers towards the back of the shop, "You have one young visitor out front."

"Just gimme a minute, Delva," replies the voice behind the wall.

I survey the appetizing display of brown-stewed chicken, roast beef, and fish on large serving plates in the showcase window. It is not yet lunchtime so there are no customers. Miss Bailey appears from the kitchen area with a large plate of small fried fish. She places the plate in the display case.

She is short but a stout woman in her sixties. She has a pleasant smile, which reveals a mouth full of straight teeth with one gold tooth on the upper right. She wears a multicolored apron around her waist and silver bangles on her left hand.

"Well, look ya, my boyfriend come look fi mi. What make you stay away so long?"

"I am busy at school," I reply meekly.

"A which school you a go? St. Georges or Kingston College?" Delva asks.

"KC ma'am."

"That nice man. Is a good school dat. You know how many pickney woulda like go there?"

"Him did win one scholarship from country—St. Ann," Miss Bailey explains.

"Him look like one nice young man. Keep up with your studies, you hear?"

"Yes, Ma'am."

"A plenty pickney a go a high school now you know. Since independence, the government open up the big school dem to ordinary people."

"Well, a Norman Manley did start to do that a few years ago before we get independence. It used to be only backra pickney dem could afford to go a secondary school," explains Miss Bailey. Backra is a Caribbean term for white people especially in reference to slave owners. Previously, the cost of a secondary education was prohibitive, so most Jamaicans had very little schooling beyond the elementary level.

"Better must come one day. No so dem say? Too much 'sufferation' a gwaan," says Delva.

"Me have something for your mother but it across the street at the apartment. Gimme a minute and we can go get it," says Miss Bailey.

Miss Bailey lives at 19 ¾ Wildman Street. At least that is what is on the gate. Next door is a small shop where you can buy peeka pow, a Chinese game of chance. It is an illegal but popular game with daily winners. Two men are at the counter stamping their bets.

Once inside the gate, there is a large two story house that is divided into several apartments rented to different families. Each apartment has only one room. There is a concrete building behind the house which serves as a common kitchen. Beside that is a smaller structure with showers and toilets. Between these two buildings is a concrete cistern and a vertical pipe with running water and a spigot. It is called a standpipe-it appears to stand upright from the ground.

Miss Bailey's apartment is a large room at the front of the house. We enter it from a wide verandah that spans the entire front of the house. The first thing I notice is the clean and shiny hardwood floor. I am afraid to walk on it; it is so polished. The room boasts some expensive and stylish furniture—a large chifforobe, a china cabinet, a chest of drawers and a dining table. Everything is spotless.

She pulls opens a drawer and retrieves a rum bottle. I can tell she doesn't want me to see it. Before I can get a good look, she carefully wraps it in newspaper, puts it in a bag and hands it to me.

"Tek this to your mother for me. Careful with it. Go straight home and don't stop and play."

A week later, I am at Miss Bailey's early on a Saturday morning. Delva explains that she is not there but expected at any moment.

"She gone a Coronation market to buy up some supplies."

"She is one busy woman," I add with a smile.

"Yeah man, she do de work of three smaddy. Miss Bailey, no 'fraid to work, she working hard from she young. Her madda did have plenty pickney and dem father did left dem. So, she did have fi left school early to help plant yam, banana and cocoa and sell dem inna market. You know say, nobody can count money like she. Is country market she learn 'bout money."

Just then Miss Bailey and a man appear carrying a basket and several bags of produce. I rush to help with the bags. We unload a cornucopia of pumpkin, green scallions, thyme, okras, green bananas, tomatoes, lettuce, and cabbage.

"Me did get some good bargains today. It pay to go market early."

"Me just passing, but stop to say howdy," I explain.

"Stephen, you know me always glad to see you." She quietly slips a coin into my hand. "Tell your mother hello."

I say goodbye and continue on my way feeling happy now that I have a coin in my pocket. My mother's wisdom is paying dividends. She always told me walking for nothing is always better than staying in one place for nothing.

The next time I visit Miss Bailey, she has moved her shop around the corner from the previous location. Her shop is much bigger now with a large room for dining. Her food display cabinet is also much larger and wider. It is now a small restaurant complete with signage and lighting. It is now Miss Bailey's Country Kitchen.

When will I ever get to sample her oxtail and cow-foot dishes, I wonder? It is dinner time and workmen are streaming in to eat after a hard day's work. Miss Bailey and Delva are busy serving dishes of stew peas and rice, curry chicken, and saltfish and callaloo. Someone orders a box of Foska oats and a cup of hot water. I recognize him as a young man from my district in St. Ann. I was told I might see him here as this is where he eats dinner every day. I wave to him and he waves back.

"Stephen, a soon come yuh hear. Go and play with those boys outside until I get a break, Miss Bailey says as she waves to me.

I exit through a side door from the shop into a typical tenement yard consisting of sub-standard dwellings jammed close together on a single plot of land. The occupants share resources like running water and toilets. Four boys are playing a game of Ludo, another group is playing checkers. I lean against a wall to watch. Suddenly all eyes are on the gate. Two young pretty girls in their high school uniforms are coming towards us.

"Peter, your girlfriend a come fi visit you," whispers one of the boys jokingly.

"A joke you a make."

"Dem girls not interested in boys, is only books them care 'bout.'"

"Leave the people dem daughter alone," proclaims another boy.

"Is Jasmine that in the Wolmer's blue and Carol in St. Hugh's green uniform. Dem live in here."

"Girls from tenement yard going to good school now," explains one boy.

The girls walk slowly by. I pretend not to see them, but I notice that Jasmine looks in my direction and smiles ever so faintly. My heart skips a beat as I force myself to look at the board games as if I didn't see her.

Peter wins the Ludo game. He stands up and declares that he must go home now. The boys point to the box he was sitting on and ask me, "Stephen, you wanna play?" I nod and take the seat.

I play two games and come close to winning once. Miss Bailey calls out to me and I give up my seat and go to her. The dinner crowd has thinned out and there are empty tables in the dining room. She asks if I would like some brown stew chicken and rice and peas. I quickly accept and she goes to prepare a plate for me.

"How is school?" she shouts from the kitchen area.

"It's fine." I yell back.

"My generation did not get much schooling. Plus, we head did dunce and teacher beat we. Me did leave school early. Me couldn't take the big lick dem every day. If you no answer quick, quick, teacher ready with the strap fi lick you."

"My mother say to tell you howdy. She coming to see you next week."

"A long time me no see her. Why she stay so. After me no do her nothin'."

"She busy with the new baby." I offer as an excuse.

"She no can walk with the baby. A little breeze-out good for dem you know?"

"Yes, Miss Bailey, I will tell her."

"And you don't be so scarce either. This Kingston life not easy. We country people have fi stick together."

"Is which part a country you from Miss Bailey?"

"Me come from St. Mary. Twenty years ago me come to Kingston. Me couldn't get no work, so me start selling fruit and vegetables outside a Missa Chin shop. Him did give me a small space under him piazza. One day me had some fry dumpling for me lunch and people ask to buy dem from me so me did start selling dumplings. Then me join in a "pardner" and me get first "draw" and use the money to open this shop.

A Partner system is an informal saving method in Jamaica whereby a group of individuals contribute a set amount of money regularly for a given time. Members of the group take turns withdrawing the total amount collected each period until every member has had a turn. The person who gets the first draw is basically getting an interest free loan for the duration.

"It did really rough at first but people like my food and word of mouth spread. Now customers a come from all over Kingston to eat."

"Rahtid, that is great Miss Bailey." I quickly devour the plate of food she gives me. She offers me some fruit punch to wash it down. Then she hands me a large envelope.

"Me can't see so good these days. Beg you read this fi me."

"It is from the Royal Bank of Canada. It says you have not made a transaction in twelve months. Your balance is two thousand pounds."

"Is me retirement money dat. Me will have fi make a deposit soon or dem will say the account inactive."

She puts away the papers and prepares a package of food for me to take to my mother. She reaches into the pocket of her apron and quietly slips me several coins. As I leave, she says, "come back soon, you hear?"

It is another week before I see Miss Bailey again. I join the boys playing Ludo and checkers. I finally win a game. I look forward to going to the cold supper shop now and the frequency of my visits increases. I also finally work up the courage to speak to Jasmine. We are at the same grade level and we compare notes and discuss homework issues. She is good company, and I am happy to be around her.

Each time I am at the shop, Miss Bailey asks how my mother is doing. And she always asks me to read a bill, a letter, or something for her. This time she has a stack of documents waiting for me to read. Business has been good, and she is opening another shop two blocks away on Charles Street. Delva will run the second shop and Miss Bailey's niece is coming from country to help her.

With the second shop, I am called into service to run errands between the two shops. This cuts into my Ludo and checkers playing time. The timing is also working against me seeing Jasmine. She now has netball practice in the evenings too. I know where her apartment is, but I am afraid to go knocking on her door because of her father. He has a stern look and speaks in an intimidating tone of voice, especially when he sees boys nearby. On the bright side, Miss Bailey gives me more money each week to help with lunch at school.

I smile at the memory of when I knew Jasmine was special. One day during the Easter vacation I had gone to Miss Bailey's earlier than usual. It was a moment of delight when I noticed that Jasmine was outside by the cistern washing clothes. I could tell she was a bit embarrassed to be doing laundry, but I offered to help her hang them out to dry. She relaxed and we had our best conversation ever. We talked about everything, our families, the foods we liked and what we wanted to do when we finished school. I had never talked with a girl like that before. When our hands touched as she handed me a piece of clothing to hang on the line, a charge raced through my body. My head swam from the force of it. I felt like I was on cloud nine. The moment didn't last though..Bemusedly, I watched as her father suddenly came walking through the gate. He didn't say a word but he gave her a look that made her follow him inside their apartment. I walked in a daze, back to Miss Bailey's shop, wondering what had just happened.

Now, after a hard week of school and errands, I am getting ready for bed but feel like I am coming down with something, my throat is itchy, and I am feeling warm. My mother instructs me to lie down as she goes to fix me something. She returns with a mixture of honey and lime in a glass. I take several spoons of it. She then fetches a rum bottle. It seems to be the same bottle Miss Bailey had given me to bring home. I notice that here is a leaf like substance in the bottle soaking in the rum. She adds a few drops to the glass and encourages me to drink it.. She then pours some onto her hand and wipes it cross my forehead, neck, and face.

"You will feel 'betta' in the morning."

"Is dat Miss Bailey rum bottle?" I ask.

"Yes, it have some herbs in it—full of medicine to make you feel betta." She tosses me a mischievous smile as she shakes the rum bottle.

"Miss Bailey is doing well with dem two shops." I state.

"Yes bredda, she a very good businesswoman. She know her stuff. She did get good training running a stall in St. Mary market."

The rum mixed with the medicinal herbs now feel like it is seeping through my forehead, straight to my brain. "Yes," I agreed in a faint voice. "She saw one opportunity and she took it. Her food smell and taste so good. Boy, she can cook."

"Let me tell you a secret. Everybody talk behind her back. Dem say she illiterate. She cannot read or write. Dem joke that she cannot tell the letter 'A' from a bull foot."

"But she know her money though," I explain.

"That she do fi true."

Six years later, I graduated and went on to the University of the West Indies to study history. Miss Bailey retired and moved back to

St. Mary where she bought a farm. I never saw Jasmine again, but I often think fondly of that tender moment we shared hanging clothes to dry in that tenement yard. I now wonder, would I ever feel that charge again? Or is it in the past...like Miss Bailey's cold supper shop.

AUTHOR'S NOTE

As Jamaicans looked overseas for opportunities due to the weak economy; they invariably had to leave their children behind. In "Old Time Christmas in Woodside," the author's mother has gone to America leaving him and his brother with their grandmother. He recalls the sights and sounds of his Jamaican childhood at the happiest time of the year. You can almost taste the rum and fruit that had been soaking for almost a year and baked into a sumptuous cake using a primitive oven. This story takes you back to an earlier time when children did not have electronic toys and life was lived mostly outdoors. The amenities were few, but the living was easy and carefree.

Old Time Christmas in Woodside

Basil Kong

Christmas 1958.

As soon as we said goodbye to the month of November, Christmas breeze start a blowing in Woodside, St. Elizabeth. I was fourteen years old and my brother Earl was thirteen. Our mother migrated to the United States when I was only four to take care of other people's pickney. As a result, we have been living with our Granny who raised us with much "brought-upsy."

Throughout the month of December, everybody is in the Christmas spirit with pep in our steps and broad smiles on our faces. We would start greeting each other with "Happy Christmas" and the predictable response was: "When it comes."

It is a time for big time cleaning as "company" is coming. My brother and I would set out to cut the grass with our machetes. Unfortunately, after one swing of the cutlass, it took a glancing blow off a rockstone and cut my foot. I was bleeding profusely but Granny just washed the blood off and applied some chickweed grass she had ground up. She then tied it with a piece of cloth. In less than ten days it was all healed leaving a scar that I still have. Even before it healed, we got back to whitewashing the stones from the road to our front steps. We also whitewashed the first three feet of the coconut trees in the yard. Next, we cut red poinsettias for the table.

The raisins and currants that had been soaking in overproof rum for several months were stirred into the batter and then baked into a delicious black fruitcake. We did not have an oven, so Granny would put the batter in our Dutch pot and place red-hot coals on top as well as under the pot. Earl and I took turns blowing the coals to keep the fire going. When the cake or the corn pone came out, Granny would holler: Hell a top, hell a bottom and halleluiah in the middle.

She also prepared roast beef and ham along with sorrel, our red Christmas punch, with plenty of ginger and white rum. Granny would get down on her knees, not only to pray but also to polish the floors, knocking the coconut brush with a rhythm we could dance to. New curtains that she sewed would go up because everything had to look spic and span for "company."

When "company" came, they took a stone and knocked on our gate and Granny would enthusiastically holler:

"Push the gate Mass Bertie. Me so glad fi see you. Happy Christmas!"

Earl and I would sit on the wooden sofa in our living room, listen to, and watch the adults talking, laughing, and eating roast beef, ham, Christmas cake and drinking sorrel. The palavering would go on for hours. But we were never allowed to interrupt grownups unless we were asked a question or to perform.

Granny would ask us to show off by spelling a difficult word, recite our times table or recite a Bible verse or poem. My favorite word to spell was Mississippi because I would spell it "M, I, crooked letter, crooked letter I, crooked letter, crooked letter I, humpback, humpback, I" and my favorite poem that I had memorized for the elocution contest in Santa Cruz, *Spanish Needle* by Claude McKay. I would stand with my hands folded in front of me and recite:

Lovely dainty Spanish needle
With your yellow flower and white,
Dew bedecked and softly sleeping,
Do you think of me tonight?

Shadowed by the spreading mango,
Nodding o'er the rippling stream,
Tell me, dear plant of my childhood,
Do you of the exile dream?

Do you see me by the brook's side
Catching crayfish 'neath the stone,
As you did the day you whispered:
Leave the harmless dears alone?

They all came for Christmas: Aunt Myra and Uncle Claudie lived down the way with our cousins, Monica, Carlen, Melvis and Donavon. Aunt Myrtle and Mr. Brown came from Kingston; Aunt Madge and Uncle Cleve came in from Mandeville; Aunt Edna, Mass Len and our cousins Neville, Yvonne, Doggie and Glen came in from Santa Cruz; Uncle John, his wife Merrie and their children Errol, Hugh, Odette, and Fay came in from Mile Gully.

They would unpredictably drive up with presents and new clothes and enjoyed the Christmas vittles. Even though we had no telephone or any means of communicating, we were always prepared for "company." According to Granny, if there was not enough food for "company," she would just add more pepper so folks would not eat as much. And, if even more people showed up, she would add even more pepper.

When the long-awaited day arrived, firecrackers would awaken us at the crack of dawn. Like African drums, they would explode in one part of the village and an answer was required from another area. Back and forth, the explosions would go for about an hour.

Granny would already be cracking a dozen eggs for egg punch. She deliberately separated the red and the white, being careful to extract the eye (germinal disk). I would be in charge of stirring the sugar and the yolks and Earl was in charge of whipping the egg whites. When the yolks and sugar was nice and creamy, Granny would pour in hot milk, add a bottle of stout, sprinkle in some cinnamon, nutmeg, finally mix in the fluffy egg whites, and serve us our Christmas breakfast. This inevitably left us pulling back our cheeks and saying *ahhh* in unison. We felt very satisfied and laughed as we sported white mustaches from the foamy punch.

Soon after the breakfast, our church choir would assemble and walk together on the road singing Christmas carols and inviting everyone they encountered to join in the sing-along. When they reached our house, we ran out on the veranda and joined in the singing:

Joy to the world, the Lord is come. Let earth receive her King.

After the choir left, it was our turn to exchange gifts. Both of us gave Granny a flask of brandy because we knew she liked to take a nip before going to bed. I gave Earl an old sock with some marbles and he gave me something I did not recognize in a paper bag.

"It looks like the bladder of a pig."

"It is, but also a balloon."

 "Blow it up nuh?"

"No, no, no, you first," I replied.

He showed me how to tie one end of the bladder and put a straw in the other end and blow it up. Sure enough, it acted like a balloon. We had many hours of fun blowing up that pig's bladder, letting out the air and blowing it up again. Later, we would cut it up, fry it with garlic, onions and scotch bonnet peppers and eat it with hard dough bread—great Christmas present!

"We don't want to be late for the Community Picnic, so put on your clothes," said Granny.

"Yes Granny," we replied in unison, now eager to enjoy the rest of the festivities.

When we got there, the picnic was in full swing. People were flying around on the merry-go round. The old World War veterans were marching in ill-fitting uniforms with wooden guns. The rhumba band was playing: Tan deh Mr. Goosy, Tan deh with people dancing—some were on stilts and some dressed up in Jonkonnu costumes. My favorite costume was the 'horsehead'.

Earl and I were looking forward to the donkey race as my strapping brother wanted to win. As soon as he jumped on, the donkey kicked up his hind legs and off came my brother with a thump to the ground.

"Oh my God, is he dead?" I ran up to him and jooked him with my finger.

"Earl, you dead? Talk to me no man."

"He's okay, he just got the wind knocked out of him," said a man nearby.

We took him into a shed. A woman put a wet towel on his forehead. I am fanning him with a cocoa leaf and crying in desperation.

"Earl, wake up no man."

He finally opens his eyes and whispers: "Me a hard man fi dead."

When he finally stood and walked out everyone applauded and big him up. We were just in time for the Maypole dance. We grabbed a ribbon along with twenty other young and old dancers and in an out we would dance until our ribbons were all wrapped up. Soon our legs were tired from all the dancing.

At the end of the day, our bellies were full from the jerk pork, grapenut ice cream, and sorrel. Christmas comes but once a year but when it comes, it brings good cheer!!

AUTHOR'S NOTE

In rural Jamaica, it is customary to start the day with a hot beverage in the morning. Those who could afford it drank coffee or green tea. Most folks drank what was available in their gardens or grew in the wild. These were referred to as "bush tea."

Peppermint and black mint were popular teas but cocoa, lime leaf, soursop leaf, lemongrass, blue vervain, hibiscus, sorrel, bissy, leaf of life, guinea hen and cerasse were some alternatives.

Interestingly, there is a soup made with sprat, a small fish of the herring family, that Jamaicans call "fish tea." This is not used as a morning beverage, however.

The "Peppermint" Lady

Glen Laman

Lulu Powell was busy in her kitchen making a breakfast of cornmeal porridge and mint tea for her family when she heard a loud knocking outside. She quickly dried her hands in a dishtowel and went to see who it was. A small group of women and children had gathered at her gate.

"Can we pick some peppermint, Auntie Lulu?" one of them asked.

"Me mother send me, she nuh have any tea and need some mint to boil for breakfast," another added.

"Ok. But unuu come and pick it for yourself, me busy, busy," Lulu responded as she opened the iron gate.

'Take one extra piece and plant it so "unuu" will have your own tree, nuh," she said in an encouraging tone.

At the side of her house, the Jamaican mint tree that had seen better days, was showing signs of abuse. It was as though a goat or other animal had been feeding on it. This plant had a woody stem and a bushy shape. The Jamaican mint is not actually a peppermint although that is what the people call it. Unlike a true peppermint plant, it can grow into a small tree several feet in height.

Every morning, people always came begging for mint at Lulu's gate. Folks would suddenly realize they had nothing to make tea that morning and they would send a child or someone else to get a piece of mint from Lulu's tree.

"The poor peppermint tree a go dead," Lulu lamented. "You know how long me a beg them fe take a piece of the mint and plant it so dem can have dem own tree and stop bother me every morning?" She shook her head in disgust. "Dem ears hard, you see."

The next morning when another set of neighbors arrived at her gate, she once again encouraged everyone to take an extra piece and plant it so they could have their own tree.

"Unuu no see dat the tree soon dead; then there will be nothing to pick," she explained in an exasperated tone.

Finally, one morning when the usual crowd had gathered, she shook her head and smiled.

"The tree is dead. Unuu kill it off. Come and look. You see, there is nothing to cut from now," she explained.

Nevertheless, she opened the gate and led them in to see the remnants of the mint tree. It was just a shell of its former self. They had stripped off all the leaves, only stems and branches remained.

The group looked at each other in consternation and with some confusion. When they shuffled away, convinced that Lulu's tree could provide no more mint, Lulu walked around her house to the backyard. There, away from prying eyes, she walked up to a flourishing mint tree she had growing in the backyard. It was lush with green leaves.

The next morning all was quiet as Lulu prepared breakfast. There was no crowd at her gate, and all was well with the world. She had a big grin on her face as she declared, "Lulu, after you no easy!" She had already picked several leaves for her tea that morning from her hidden mint tree.

This "peppermint" tree would be her secret from now on.

A week later, the word was all over the village.

"Did you hear how Miss Lulu fix the people dem. All now they cannot believe it. She shut down the morning peppermint tea."

"Serve them right. Dem take too much liberty. Bothering the woman every blessed morning saying them want tea."

"Is like them kill the goose that lay the golden egg," chimed a woman with a smile on her face.

"Me not sorry for them at all, at all," added another woman.

"Is an easy plant to grow. No work needed. Just plant a piece and watch it grow.

"I don't understand what wrong with some people. Now dem vex with the woman for dem own failing."

Lulu lived near the main road and she could see everyone who passed by. Sometimes she overheard people talking about the peppermint tree episode. She started thinking and then she got busy in her backyard garden. She had embarked on a new project. She did not say a word to anyone.

A couple weeks later, she placed a seedling box at her gate. As the folks passed she offered them a seedling. It was a young peppermint sprout complete with a patch of soil. Soon the word spread that Lulu was giving away peppermint sprouts for planting. The children came, the grown-ups came. They each took a sprout and thanked her.

Before long, scores of peppermint trees were growing all over the district. As people walked by, they gave Lulu updates on how well their peppermint plant was doing. She offered advice and encouragement as necessary.

Unwittingly, Lulu was abiding by the adage, "…give a man a fish, and you'll feed him for a day. Teach a man to fish, and you've fed him for a lifetime." She taught them how to be self-sufficient.

As a result, everyone resumed drinking peppermint tea in the mornings. This time, however, they picked from their own tree.

That is how Lulu Powell became known as The "Peppermint" Lady.

AUTHOR'S NOTE

Bailiffs work with the courts to enforce judgements in favor of property owners. They can evict people from property for failure to pay rent. They can also seize property to compensate property owners for unpaid rent.

When the bailiff shows up it can be a terrifying experience. Renters are typically unaware of what the rules are and what possessions bailiffs legally can and cannot seize.

In "The Bailiff", Delores's family initially lives in tenement housing which caters to the lower socioeconomic groups. They are the people who typically have tenuous employment and therefore at higher risk for eviction.

Frustrated by their experience with the bailiff, Delores and her husband are determined not to be in such a predicament ever again.

The Bailiff

Glen Laman

The mood in the city was one of jubilation. Despite the tropical heat, people moved with extra zip in their steps. Their spirits were high. The island of Jamaica was to become an independent nation ending over 300 years of British rule.

A Jamaican, Carole Joan Crawford had been crowned Miss World in the famous worldwide beauty competition in London. In the capital city of Kingston, huge crowds packed the sidewalks to get a glimpse of their beauty queen during the parade.

Inside Delores Brown's one room apartment on Malvern Avenue off Windward Road, there was a different feeling. And it was not good. Earlier this morning, she woke to a pounding on the door. When she opened the door, three men brandishing eviction papers marched in. She stood helplessly watching these unwanted visitors remove the furniture from her little apartment.

On the bed, her three-month-old daughter purred quietly as she preoccupied herself with a pacifier.

They took all her good furniture but thankfully, they left the beds. They had emptied the contents of the prized wardrobe and the beautiful chest of drawers and placed them on the floor along with the plates and utensils that were on her table.

The slender, balding white man said they were from Tom Russett, the landlord's bailiff. He and the two muscular black men were there to confiscate the furniture for non-payment of rent.

Dolores had never heard of the bailiff. She was in shock.

"But Lennie pay di rent. Me no understand, sah," she exclaimed in bewilderment.

"We have authorization from the court," the white man said.

"Lawd have mercy! You see me trial now."

"Derrick, Derrick! Beg you come here quick." She shouted out to her son playing in the yard.

"Yes, madda," he came running.

"Beg you run to the police station down on Elletson Road and tell Sergeant Jones dat these men taking away we furniture and we don't know what fi do," she instructed Derrick.

Derrick ran off barefooted down the avenue.

The men continued their removal of the furniture. A crowd had gathered in the street to watch the proceedings. This caused further embarrassment to poor Delores.

"What a cross!" Someone in the crowd shouted as the men hoisted the wardrobe into the truck.

"A pure wickedness a gwaan! Independence not going save we," another person exclaimed.

"Too much suffering. How long shall di wicked reign over my people?" An elderly woman in the crowd chimed in.

"A one nice piece of furniture dat. They going to sell it off quick, quick," said a young man.

As the truck drove away, the crowd quietly disperses. Delores sat on the bed, with her head in her hands, and sobbed quietly. Her baby beside her made a cooing sound and tried to reach for the soother that has fallen out of her mouth.

Delores attempted to tidy up the mess the men had made in the room. The bailiff's men had thrown all her clothes and other personal items on the floor. They had left the double bed and the tiny cot that Derrick slept on. In a corner of the room was a small box on which were containers of water and groceries plus pots and pans.

An out of breath Derrick came running through the door. "The sergeant say nothing they can do. It is a court matter," he says.

"All right me son, come help me straighten up the clothes dem."

Later that afternoon, when her common-law husband Lennie arrived home, Delores met him at the door.

"Them say you never pay the rent and Mr. Russett and him man dem take away our furniture."

"No sah. Nothing no go so. I pay Mr. Lewis the rent in cash I even have receipt," Lennie tried to explain.

"When you pay him Lennie?

"Me was one day late with the money and him say no problem."

"But you never did tell me you pay him late Lennie. What happen?"

"Remember we had to pay for the new schoolbooks for Derrick. So, we didn't have enough left over and I had to borrow from my sister."

"The whole street a laugh at we now. Is a shame, shame!" Delores retorted. "You know that when Jamaicans say no problem, it is a problem," She added.

"All right. Me soon come back, Him just live one block over from here." Lennie ducked out the door.

Delores was busy cooking rice and peas and curried chicken on the two-burner kerosene stove in a corner of the room. She fumbled with plates and utensils which were now stashed on the floor as there was no table.

Suddenly, she heard a commotion in the street as if a crowd was gathering again. Delores peeped through the window and saw a man pulling a large handcart loaded with their furniture down the middle of the street. Her heart nearly stopped when she saw Lennie walking behind the handcart. "What is this now Lord?" she exclaimed as she looked to Lennie for an explanation.

Lennie shrugged. "Mr. Lewis say is not them own the house. They only sublet it and rent out the rooms. Mr. Whitehead is the owner. Two other people pay Mr. Lewis later than me. Whitehead no get all di money on the 5th and so him file the papers with the court. By the time Lewis pay him it too late to stop the bailiff."

"A one whole heap of crosses this," exclaimed Delores. "Why we always suffer so?" Delores exclaimed.

Lenny explained what happened while he helped the handcart man and Derrick move the furniture back into their room. Derrick mostly moved the clothes and other items scattered on the floor to make room.

"No bother worry yourself," Lennie admonished his wife. "Is a good thing Mr. Lewis did have a telephone to call the bailiff, else they would have sell off our furniture before you could say Busta and Manley."

"Come make we eat some food. All dis confusion make me weak and tired," Delores gestured toward the table.

Delores dished out rice and peas and brown stew chicken onto plates. As they sat down to eat, she placed slices of tomato and a piece of lettuce on each plate. Lennie poured carrot juice into glasses and slid the glasses to Delores and Derrick."

"Everything work out, "said Lennie, wiping a film of carrot juice from his upper lip.

"No sah. We can't live in this place," Delores exclaimed. "We start looking for another place right away. How we know it won't happen again? Our life not easy, you know? Even though them talking about independence from England we still a struggle. This must never happen again." The little family remained tense and pensive for the rest of the evening, except for the happy purrs and gurgles of the infant.

The next day Lennie comes home with a stack of papers. He is excited and has a big smile on his face.

"Why you so happy?" Asked Delores.

"We have a chance to move to a better place Delores. Over on Mango Tree lane is a house with four bedrooms. We can rent two of the rooms and we pay less than what we pay now," Lennie explains.

"You must be mad no rahtid," retorts Delores. "What if we can't find nobody to rent to; answer me dat!"

"No man. We must can find two people. Think about it nuh Delores?"

"Me 'fraid fi trouble sah! Mr. Russett and him man dem make me 'fraid, 'fraid." Delores shakes her head in disagreement.

"All right then forget it, but we have to move still," says Lennie with a sigh.

No more is said on the matter and they eat dinner and listen to RJR radio before going to bed. Lennie is careful to not bring up the subject again.

A couple days later, Delores takes her daughter to visit her cousin Verna in Rollington Town. Her cousin is living with a bus driver for the Kingston Bus Company everybody calls "Jolly Joseph." He works odd hours and Verna has discovered that he meets a lot of women on his bus route and is having several relationships. She wants to leave him badly. Delores gets an idea.

That evening when Lennie comes home, she is anxious to discuss Verna's predicament but she waits until after dinner.

"Verna is leaving Charles."

"She should a left him long time. Him is a wanderer." Says Lennie.

"Well, she needs a place to move and I was thinking about that house you were talking about... She has a good job and is very reliable."

"You mean it? My friend Winston need a place too. Make we do it nuh!" Lennie said excitedly. "Me going to see the owner of the Mango Tree house tomorrow after work then."

They work out a favorable deal with the owner and the next month they all move in together.

Two Months Later

Delores and Lennie are now living in a rented house with Cousin Verna and another tenant. Delores can add to their savings account each month with some of what they save on their portion of the rent. They hear of another house that is available for rent and Delores wants to get it and then rent out the rooms.

"Me no know if we can chance it, Delores. It too risky," says Lennie. "Plenty people take chance and lose dem shirt, you know?"

"Nuthin' ventured nothing gained. That's what my madda always say," quips Delores.

"Well, coward man keep sound bone," counters Lennie.

"Make we strike while the iron is hot," says Delores.

"All right then. Cross you finger dem. I will go look at the house right away," says Lennie.

The next day they sign the lease for a second house and put the word out that there are rooms for rent.

"It look like it might work, Delores. Two people interested in rooms already," said Lennie, smiling and rubbing his palms together then cracking his knuckles.

Three Years Later

Lennie and Delores are sitting in their living room, in a new house, on a new sofa watching their new Sylvania 19-inch TV with rabbit ears antenna. Their daughter is sitting on the floor playing with her toys. In the kitchen, Lorna their helper is preparing dinner. Their son Derrick has just come home from playing lawn tennis.

Lorna opens the new refrigerator and reaches for a jug. "You want me to serve lemonade or sorrel with the dinner, Miss Delores?"

"I think we can have some wine tonight. We are celebrating a new house we just rented out," replies Delores.

"Okay, I will open a bottle. Is how many house you have now, Miss?" asks Lorna.

"This is our fourth one. That's why Lennie is so busy these days keeping up with the properties," says Delores with a smile. "Nuff tings happen since our daughter born. We took a chance and rented our first house. It wasn't easy, but now we have four. The Lord been good to us. Thank you, Jesus."

"That is a good story, Miss," said Lorna. "Oh, me just remember, one man did call for Mas Lennie today, Miss. Him name Tom Russett."

"Okay. Thank you for the message. We use him occasionally. He is the landlord bailiff," says a smiling Delores.

"Oh, that is the same man who come and take people furniture if them don't pay rent?" asks Lorna.

"Yes, is him same one. One day when we have time I will tell you the story of how I first met the bailiff," says Delores with a secret smile.

AUTHOR'S NOTE

*It is a reality that some men will stray from the marital bed.
However, it is unusual for a Jamaican woman to allow her
man this freedom without complaint. In Ruby's Love Story,
she believes that dogs are always going to bark and bite,
and men will always find ways to satisfy their sexual desires.
So why fuss and fight over something that is so natural to
them? "If you get rid of all the arguments about sex with
other women, you can rid yourself of ninety percent of the
arguments in your marriage." Oh, if it could be that easy!*

Ruby's Love Story

Basil Kong

When Jerome was fourteen years old, several girls were already in love with him. Some even wrote him poems which they slipped into his pockets. However, he only had eyes for Ruby, a pretty girl from the neighboring town of Brighton.

She had a good heart, a sweet spirit, and a keen sense of justice. The romance started when he was shaking her hand during the ceremonies on Sports Day. As he tickled the middle of her hand, she squeezed his thumb, which he took as a signal that she liked him as well.

Her spirit just took to him. As the daughter of rigid, puritanical parents, she was serious about her studies and dressed modestly. She did not even wear a bangle or pierced earrings like the other girls and her face reflected the sweetness and sincerity of her spiritual nature.

When they talked, she wanted to know how him "take lick so" from his teachers as she thought it was intolerably painful when she took licks in her palms or when her father peppered her ankle with a switch. Jerome was her hero, but she made it abundantly clear to him not to try anything as she was not about to "do it" with any boy.

"What you take me for? I respect my sisters. I am only trying to keep your company," he proclaimed.

And so, Jerome settled on walking her home whenever the opportunity presented itself, especially when he attended Boy's Brigade meetings. This was where he learned to tie knots with ropes, study the Bible, drill like soldiers, compete in sports, and practice survival strategies. She attended "Upward and Onward" after school on Wednesdays at the Moravian Church where she learned cooking and sewing as well as other homemaking skills.

They talked often about God and religion. His resistance and protest against religion notwithstanding, she remained steadfast in her faith. He would try to convince her that "God has nothing to do with religion."

"I love a God that loves and protects me, the more I praise and honor him, the more I am blessed. That's all. For non-believers, heathens and infidels like you, no proof of His existence and His church is ever enough, while the faithful like me don't need proof and don't question."

"I don't mean to argue" he said, "but there is no virtue in ignorance. We should all seek truth."

"But Jerome, there is no truth. One man's bread is another man's poison. Every time someone, even my teachers tell me something, I find that the opposite can also be true. So, to me, truth is whatever each of us believe."

He was impressed with her logic and how eloquently she expressed herself. He had underestimated her all along. It was like sunshine after a rain. He had found someone he could talk with on a high level. In his excitement, he was like a gushing spring trying to discuss other things he had been thinking about.

On one of these walking and talking occasions, he happened to see an anthill, and once the idea fell into his brain, he could not help himself, so he guided Ruby to sit down and talk with him. In the minute after unwittingly sitting in the ants' nest, she started to get stings and cried out in distress, repeatedly saying, "Jesus Christ, Jesus Christ, Jesus Christ."

She instantly stripped off all her clothes, and he helped as best he could by slapping the ants from all over her body. He felt a thrill in his groin and soon found himself tormented with desire as something very hard came up between them. But it was no use.

Ruby yelled out, "You sadistic brute! You too bad!" and pushed him into the pond creating a big splash; shucked the ants from her clothes before putting them back on and running away. While Ruby ran off, he remained in the cold water until his tempest cooled. He eventually stopped panting like a dog but laughed with evil joy as he made his way home.

When Ruby got home, she reflected on what "that bad boy" did to her and had a good laugh over it herself. In fact, she couldn't help thinking how exciting it was for her, and it came to her in her dreams that they were "doing it" that night. On her way to school the following day, she pulled some "love weed" and yelled, "Jerome," spat on it and threw it over her shoulder. It landed on some cerasee bush growing by the side of the road. A week later, the entire bush was glowing with the yellow threads of gold. It made her feel happy and she knew then she would marry him some day.

Jerome turned fifteen years old and had to leave school as that was the extent of public education in Jamaica at that time. He never had a birthday party or knew how old he was at any particular time, so it was a shock when the headmaster came to tell him that he could not return to school. This development was a great relief to the headmaster, several teachers and fellow students who could finally exhale.

As he and Ruby were the same age, she was also leaving elementary school at the same time but she was hired to assist her mother as a pretrained pupil teacher at St. Elizabeth Technical School for two years. From there, she enrolled in Shortwood Teacher's College between 1973 and 1976, passed the exams to receive a teaching certificate, and started teaching at Barking Lodge All Age School.

Jerome moved to Cuba and joined Castro's army. He was sent to the war in Angola where he fought against the white South Africans. When he came back to Jamaica years later, he was staying at the home of his Aunt Beryl before deciding on his next move. He had often thought of Ruby over the years and was eager to see her. He learned that she was sick with the Dengue fever and was being cared for by her parents in Brighton.

Once a member of the household caught the fever, it quickly spread to everyone else and the entire family felt poorly. Feeling invincible and fearing neither man nor germ, Jerome bought both his driver's license and an SUV with some of the money he had brought back from Cuba.

He made his way to St. Elizabeth battling the bad roads and set about nursing Ruby with affectionate devotion. His presence was the medicine the family needed as she quickly recovered along with the rest of her family. He was like a breath of fresh air that blew in to cool their fevers.

When he slept at his parent's old house, he marveled at how much it had shrunk. He could not believe that it used to comfortably accommodate over six people when he was a child and how claustrophobic he now felt in it as a man. He went daily to hold Ruby's hand, wipe her fevered brow with a damp cloth and tell her stories about the Angolan war from which he recently returned. No one in Jamaica knew that he had volunteered to be a guerilla fighter in Africa.

Soon word got around that Jerome, the impetuous young soldier, was back from war. During his long absence, the good citizens of

Woodside had been guessing as to whether he was dealing drugs, in prison or worse. They gathered with eager ears and drank up the liquor he bought as well as listened to his every word. He had returned eight years later, apparently flush with cash. They now thought him an angel in disguise with the expectation that he would rescue them from their misery with his promises of work. They hoped and prayed nightly for someone to come along and revitalize a village that was languishing. Jerome, ever faithful to where his navel string was buried, felt at home in Woodside.

While he received no recognition from politicians, he was satisfied with the respect and affection he was receiving from Ruby as well as the people of Woodside. Ruby was a good Christian girl who was expected to retain her virginity until she was married, so no intimacy had existed between them. But one lonely night he was in Woodside struggling and even trembling with delusions of the passion between them and feeling the need for female companionship, he drove to Brighton with sinful fire in his belly to see the love of his life. He parked the car several chains away and walked on stone steps in the soft moonlight through the cane piece with the long leaves brushing against his face.

Upon reaching Ruby's wooden bedroom window, he tapped on it excitedly. She opened it and was glad to see him. He quickly climbed in and was in a sweet embrace when her father came to her door and demanded to know who was in her room.

Ruby tried to push him out of the window but although embarrassed by the lack of dignity in the situation he said, "No sah, me nah make no man run me. Open the door." So, Ruby opened the door and her father told Jerome that visitors to his home usually use the front door and declared in no uncertain terms that he was no longer welcome in his house.

"Mr. Duncan, with all due respect sah, me love you daughter and want to marry her."

Her father knew about Jerome's chronic reputation for womanizing.

"So, you plan to marry me daughter. Let me ask you a simple straight forward question: can you promise me and her that you will give up all your other women and be faithful only to her?"

Jerome swallowed his spit even though his mouth was already dry and told Ruby that he already had two children and he was not going to lie.

"I don't believe I could stop seeing other women even under the best of circumstances."

"Jerome, as much as I love you, I don't think we can have a life together," Ruby responded.

"I have nothing against you, but I oppose the marriage because you are not a one-woman man and you would only end up making me daughter miserable. Good night sir," her father then said.

Things had not turn out the way he imagined. He humbly high-tailed it back to his car with a deflated ego and made his way to Woodside as a frustrated and unfortunate creature. The feeling of dishonor, loneliness and embarrassment was enormous. After making it back to his parent's house and sleeping it off, he left for Kingston the next day brokenhearted.

In the ensuing five years, he would have no contact with Ruby and neither of them found true love with anyone else. Then just as she was about to board a city bus to make her way home from her teaching duties, she heard a voice, "Chickie, don't mount the bus!" It was the voice of her long-lost love. She turned from the bus, grinning with excitement, waved at him, ran back down the platform against the flow of the embarking passengers, met his open arms and hugged him with a determination that almost suffocated both of them. She then parted her lips to receive the kiss she had longed for.

Ruby had thought of Jerome often over the years as other relationships with men had been dismal failures. She had met many men who were not what they appeared to be, who were deceptive and who only feigned affection for her. She had grown to detest men who were too cautious, fretful and who constantly worried about life's insecurities and dangers. She called them "fraidy, fraidy men." Despite his flaw, Jerome was a "real' man.

She remembered how fearless and manly Jerome was and compared them to him. She confessed, "I have been miserable and wanted to find you. Everywhere I go, I search the crowd looking for your face and longing for a moment like this." He told her that there will never be another woman for him. As low as his spirits were, he was much pleased and immediately felt cheered and refreshed. From that fateful day, their hearts regained their joy and they were committed to each other. They spent the evening over a wonderful meal at her house in Portmore, catching up on the past five years, laughing, and delighting in each other's company. They were both now twenty-nine years old.

In anticipation of the pleasures of a happy home, they quickly set a date for their marriage. With this new commitment, he wrote to his parents in England with the good news as well as made their way to Brighton and Woodside to visit family and friends all for the sake of finally receiving their family's blessings.

But several of Ruby's family, suspicious of the source of his wealth and his womanizing, tried to impede their impending union. "He will leave you with pickney and no support." Aunt Beryl, on the other hand, was delighted with the news and started making plans for the wedding immediately. She adored Ruby. His promise to all who doubted him as marriage material was, "I don't drink, I don't smoke, and I don't go a road." It was not by accident that he left out any mention of his other women who he continued to see even as his marriage plans were being made.

He had one of the diamonds that he had brought back from Angola made into an engagement ring and inspired by his deep thoughts, wrote a poem for the occasion. As he was visiting her after she was already prepared for sleep, he sat on a chair beside her bed and recited by heart,

Chickie Sweetheart, Darling,
the love I have to offer you is pure and strong
It has nothing of false intention to lull you with lies or
illusion
I want to see you happy,
completely happy—in a settling frame of quality.
And I believe you are too sincere to reject my offer.
I want to see you free, basically free from unconscious
conflict.
And today, once again, I offer my love to you that will
lead us to matrimony.
Will you marry me?

She was impressed, but she was much too practical to get mushy and sentimental, "Jerome, cut the bull, I have no illusions that marrying you is going to be easy. Against the advice of my family, I agree to marry you because me weak fi you. But I am going to fasten my seatbelt because I know it's going to be a bumpy ride. If you receive me as I am with all my deficiencies and misguided opinions, I will receive you as you are as well." So, he placed the diamond ring on her finger and she lifted the sheet that covered her body and invited Jerome to take off his clothes and join her.

The ecstasy was beyond description. With his head pillowed between her breasts, they spent the rest of the night and the following day in bed. They had finally found each other and were happy. Their life grew happier with each passing day. He was now her man and she accommodated herself in every way to his needs and preferences. When he visited her obviously reeking of another woman's odor, she asked him, "Were you with another woman?" His answer was "Yes. And you are next. If you take care of the banana, the banana will take care of you."

They married on August 22, 1983 at the Richmond Park Moravian Church with the Rev. Justin Peart presiding. While her father continued to harbor doubts about Ruby's decision, she was now thirty, living on her own and could make her own decisions. Many an eye was blurred with tears of happiness as she vowed to celebrate each anniversary and recall these happy memories each year without regret.

The beautiful wedding was followed by a reception at Devon House where the wine and spirits flowed. The food was delicious. Jerome was happy and exclaimed, "Me belly full and me heart full!" The congratulatory speeches went on much too long as usual.

There were so many unsteady feet trying to dance that one guest even suggested that the only difference between a Jamaican wedding and a Jamaican funeral was one less drunk. His parents came all the way from England and his older Brother Patrick who had migrated to the United States came back for the occasion.

It was a fine family reunion for many people who had not seen each other for a long time.

AUTHOR'S NOTE

Jamaicans of a certain age can recall growing up in an era when people did not have to secure their doors at night. Many houses did not even have locks back then. Crime was a rare occurrence. This all changed in the decades after the island gained independence as the crime rate skyrocketed. The number of murders went from less than 80 per year to hundreds in the decades to follow.

This development was scary to everyone but especially terrifying to those who had lived overseas while this transformation was taking place. In "The Hero of Fern Gully," three visiting siblings become stranded on a country road at night. It is against this backdrop that a mysterious stranger comes to their rescue.

The Hero of Fern Gully

Glen Laman

The small Hyundai sedan is struggling uphill along the narrow winding road through the Fern Gully. It is heading towards the town of Moneague and away from the resort town of Ocho Rios. Behind the Hyundai, a stream of headlights beam on the small vehicle as the driver turns off the air conditioning in the hope that its tiny engine would generate a little more power.

Neville is driving. He is accompanied by his two sisters, Cherry and Blossom. They are visiting from America to celebrate their grandma's 97th birthday, which they feel could be her last.

It was almost as if Neville could feel the impatience of the drivers behind him. The need to get off the dark, treacherous road is palpable in the intermittent hum of the cars behind him. He could understand that they were no doubt anxious to return to the city of Kingston after a weekend on the North Coast.

As Neville skillfully navigates around a sharp curve, the car narrowly misses a pothole—that scourge of the Jamaican road. Neville stifles an expletive, sparing his sisters who had now become concerned at the intense darkness of the gully's roadway.

The Fern Gully is a former riverbed that has been converted into a roadway. The trees and variety of ferns form a natural winding tunnel for several miles. It is considered one of Jamaica's natural beauty spots.

The siblings had left Runaway Bay while it was still daylight hoping to return to Claremont before dark. To their dismay, they discover that the main road via St. Ann's Bay is impassable because of flood damage from Hurricane Ivan the previous year. To get to their destination, they made a detour several miles and approach their destination via the town of Golden Grove.

As the car rounds a corner, the intense darkness recedes as they have come to the end of the Fern Gully and the road is wider. The lighter darkness of night is a welcome development. The cars behind them increased their speed. Many zoom past the Hyundai as the road straightens. Suddenly, there is a bang, then a reverberation as their car hits a pothole.

Seconds later, the "plop, plop, plop" of a busted flat tire and the realization of a nightmare: a flat tire at night on a lonely country road.

Neville pulls over to the side of the road. There is no flashlight. As fear grips the occupants, Cherry asks, "Is it wise to stop here? Let's keep going!"

"There is nothing for miles, to keep driving will just make it worse. It will wreck the rim," Neville replies.

He jumps out of the car. Cherry and Blossom follow.

"Look for some stones to block the wheels," said Neville.

"Maybe we should look for something to defend ourselves," says Blossom in an ominous voice.

"Yes, we hear too much story about the crime rate," says Cherry.

Fumbling in the dark, Neville manages to replace the flat tire with a spare. Relieved, they all pile back into the car and take off.

Alas! After driving a few hundred yards, they hear another alarming "plop, plop, plop." A flat tire again. They stop and examine the just replaced tire and realize that it is completely flat. Evidently, the spare is defective.

They have been staying in Claremont where they grew up. Nothing looks like it did when they were growing up there years ago. Drastic changes have been made and it's very surprising to see grills or burglar bars encased around every house. Crime and corruption are all they are hearing in the news. Most of the people they once knew are living abroad or in Kingston.

Being stranded on a dark lonely road with no streetlight on a Sunday night is not a comforting thought. If only the government had fixed the roads, they would not have had to make the detour.

"What a disaster! Not just one, but two flat tires. Where can you fix a tire on a Sunday evening?" Neville reaches for the borrowed cell phone and calls Steve, one of the few friends for whom they have a contact number, but Steve is out of town. He offers to call someone to help.

The car is in a dangerous spot on a narrow road with no shoulder. Cars zoom by and it feels like someone will run into them at any moment. Neville decides to move the car to a better location and he drives slowly on the flat tire. With each turn of the wheel, the tire is being chewed up. Meanwhile, the Sunday night traffic picks up and they witness several near accidents from their car.

Minutes later, they are on the secondary road that runs through Orange Park and connects with the main road in Golden Grove three kilometers from their destination.

Neville brings the Hyundai to a final stop on the paved shoulder of the turnoff. All they can do now is sit and wait. Blossom calls grandma's house and Dolly, her helper, answers. She explains they will be late because of their predicament. Moments later, Steve calls back to say his friend, Troy, is on the way to assist them.

They weigh the options. The car is a rental from Montego Bay—there is no way they can leave it overnight were they to get a ride home. But where to get a new tire? The flat on the car is now completely ruined. Where is AAA when you need them?

Peering into the dark night, Neville glances at his watch but couldn't see his own hand much less the watch. He starts up the engine and looks at the bright dashboard. "9 o'clock," he mumbles to no one in particular. He reclines his seat and listens to the sound of crickets outside, while worry and fear grips the occupants inside the car.

Suddenly, screeching tires cause everyone to jump up in alarm. Beams from the headlamps illuminated the path as the other car stops alongside them. A young man hops out. "Me come fe help with de flat tire," he says.

Everyone released a collective sigh of relief. Neville opens the door and shakes the other man's hand, "What you name, sah?"

"Ian."

This does not compute; Steve had said someone named Troy would be coming.

"Where you come from Ian?"

Ian says he is from Golden Grove and was sent by a guy he only knows as "Pops." This story does not match up with what they are expecting.

Can they trust this stranger?

Ian senses their hesitation.

He suggests they use his spare and retrieves it from his trunk. It is the same size as the Hyundai, but the lugs do not match up. Ian says there is a tire place in Ocho Rios that is open Sundays. But how do they proceed?

"Me not going in that car," whispers Cherry.

"Me neither," adds Blossom.

Neville doesn't want to leave his sisters alone with the car.

Ian volunteers to remain with the Hyundai while they take his Toyota Camry to find a tire. That seems reasonable and they quickly accept his offer. After exchanging cell phone numbers, they head back towards Fern Gully and Ocho Rios.

A few minutes later, Ian calls to tell them that his car is low on gas and they should get some in Ocho Rios. They find a gas station and fill the tank. The tire store is in a place called Exchange between Ocho Rios and Oracabessa.

After driving around and not finding the tire store, they return to the gas station for directions. Finally, they locate the tire shop but it's closed for the night.

It is now 10 pm. They call Ian. He is out of ideas but says he is hungry and asks that they buy him some food on the way back.

The situation is not looking good. The night is getting late. The cell phone rings. A relative from the US is calling. They explain the problem and realize the phone is running out of credits. Now they have to get a new phone card.

They stop at several shops, but none sell the "Reddi Celli" card they need as it is an older type. They spot a large gas station that is still open, and they pull in. Luckily, they have the correct phone card for sale. Neville asks if anyone knows where he can get tires at this time of night. Everyone says no.

Just then, an elderly man walks into the gas station and buys a Coke and a penny bun.

The cashier asks him if he knows a tire place that would be open at this time of night. He says yes, there is a place out by Mammee Bay where they are open 24 hours. It is a yellow building on the left side near where the road is all dusty and rough due to the construction of the new highway to Montego Bay.

Neville thanks him and heads back to the borrowed Toyota. He repeats the news to his sisters. "What are the chances there is a 24-hour tire repair shop in this part of the island?"

"I can't think of one in the U.S. either," Cherry quips.

But there is no other option. They head off to Mammee Bay and find themselves in the middle of road construction. The asphalt had been ripped up and a choking and blinding white dust makes driving difficult. They do not see the tire shop but notice a side road after they pass it. Turning around, they go up the hill and onto the side street stopping to ask a man standing on the corner: "Do you know where the 24-hour tire shop is?"

"Yah, Mon. It just down deh so. But you have fe drive pon de lickle piece a road bank fe get deh,"

"What did he say?" asked Blossom.

"It's nearby, but we will need to use the narrow-elevated shoulder to get there," Neville explains. The women laugh.

In widening the road, the construction crew had dug away most of a narrow side road that runs about five feet above the main road creating a mini precipice. This is the only way to get to the tire shop. So Neville slowly and cautiously maneuvers the Toyota on this side road.

After a few breathless moments, they reach the tire shop. And it does say, "24 Hour Tyre Repair" on the sign. Two men are sleeping in a tree. Three dogs approach to investigate. One of the men, Leroy, stirs as the car approaches. He explains he has no tires but can fix flats.

"Ok I have two tires for repair then," says Neville.

Leroy points out that the rim is bent and needs to be fixed first. He springs into action and begins working the first flat tire, knocking at the rim with a hammer. Once the rim is sufficiently round, he applies a black paste to the portion of the tire that meets the wheel and inflates it—but it does not hold the air.

He tries again but still no luck. Neville suggests he try the other wheel from the spare tire. The tire on this wheel is all torn up, but the wheel Leroy says, appears fixable and works on it. This time the tire maintains the air pressure and everyone sighs with relief.

After paying for the repair, they are happy to make their way back to the dusty main road toward Ocho Rios. Everyone is hungry, so they make a stop at the Jerk Center and buy several orders of jerk chicken with rice and peas before heading back through Fern Gully.

At a little past midnight, the traffic is virtually nonexistent. Neville turns off the lights for a second to appreciate the density of the darkness beneath the canopy of ferns. Swarms of fireflies, known as peenie-wallies, provide an ethereal backdrop, twinkling overhead and gliding in between the tall trees of Fern Gully.

"It's like we're in another world," whispers Cherry, in awe.

They took a moment to absorb the wonder of their surroundings. Neville turns on his high beam and revs the engine to continue on their way.

A tired and hungry Ian is waiting with the Hyundai when they pull up. They give him some food and he quickly devours the jerk chicken. Hurriedly, they put on the tire. It works! Hallelujah!

After giving Ian a very big tip and thanking him profusely, the weary travelers head to Claremont, driving carefully, as they have no spare tire. Soon after, they reach Grandma's house.

Back in the US, the three siblings share the amazing story of that night on the Fern Gully road. And, in their telling, Ian became The Hero of Fern Gully.

AUTHOR'S NOTE

The roaming music man is the proverbial traveling musician who wanders the countryside with his banjo or guitar conquering the hearts of vulnerable maidens. He often leaves disaster in his wake. While this situation is unfortunate, Jamaican women are strong and resilient or as the saying goes, able to "tun hand and make fashion." In this story, Enid suffers rejection after rejection for her indiscretion but somehow manages to survive and thrive against the odds.

The Legacy of the Roaming Music Man

Basil Kong

In 1968, Enid Stewart was a bright fifteen-year-old at Springfield All Age School. According to Marjorie Newsome, her favorite teacher, in addition to completing all her assignments, she always took at least one first place in the annual elocution contests for elementary school children in Santa Cruz each year. Enid enjoyed memorizing poems and Bible passages.

The reports sent home always made her parents proud and neighbors were forever reminding them about what a good girl Enid was and how their pickney have manners. She was also the girls' sports champion. Enid was the Stewart's only child and they just knew she had a promising future.

Her parents could not afford to send her to High School when she left Elementary School and so she accepted Ms. Aggie's offer to apprentice as a seamstress/dressmaker in her shop. She was able to make a little money and stay at home under the watchful eye of her parents.

Saturday was Enid's favorite day because she helped her mother make delicious red pea soup with corn-pork and dumplings. After enjoying lunch with her parents, Enid would take a tureen of this wonderful soup to her grandmother who lived a mile away in Donegal.

Halfway to her destination, she heard someone singing in the distance. Being curious, she waited for the singer to catch up to her. She was immediately smitten by the handsome minstrel who looked to be at least twenty-five years old, dressed in a sea blue jacket over a crisp white shirt with ruffles. He even had a peacock feather in his hat and a guitar strapped to his back. When he saw her, he smiled broadly.

"Good afternoon young lady, I cannot believe my luck."

"What do you mean?"

"An angel wearing the most beautiful red dress just fell from the sky right in front of me. So, where are you going pretty lady?"

Enid's palm started to sweat. Her face flushed and her heart was beating out of her chest. She never heard such flattery.

"You are without a doubt the most beautiful girl I have ever set my eyes on."

"Thank you for saying that sir," she replied.

"But are you a bad girl?"

"I don't know what you mean sir."

I mean, are you beautiful and desirable?"

"If you say so sir."

"Why are you in such a hurry?"

"I am taking soup for me granny. She is expecting me."

"Your presence has given me so much pleasure, can I at least sing you a song?"

She hesitated.

"I promise it won't take long." He took off his jacket and placed it on the ground.

"Here, sit."

When she put down the tureen food carrier and sat on his jacket, he longingly admired her long legs glistening from the coconut oil she rubbed on them earlier.

"I cannot stay too long," she reminded him.

She was mesmerized when he serenaded her with sweet romantic songs then slid down gently next to her and continued singing softly in her ears. She was giddy with laughter and did not resist as he kissed her and slowly pulled up her dress. He was everything she dreamed of and she gave in to her irresistible urges as he sang,

"Carry mi ackee go a Linstead market, not a quattie worth sell," he crooned in a breathtaking voice, pausing to nip her ear

They were passionate in their lovemaking on his jacket, on the ground, under the breadfruit tree. He took her virginity and was gone. His parting words were "Take care of yourself." In his haste, he forgot his jacket. She decided to keep it as a souvenir. She did not even know his name. The pain felt good. But while she felt happy, she also felt scared and confused and couldn't make sense out of what just happened. With her eyes closed, she laid on her back for a minute gathering her thoughts unable to wipe the smile from her face. She then hurriedly got up and ran the rest of the way to her grandmother's house. Granny asked why she was late, and she merely said: "Sorry Granny. I met a minstrel music man on the way and stopped to listen to some of his beautiful songs." "I hope that is all he did." Granny replied.

On her way home she decided that this was going to be her secret. She folded up and hid the blue Jacket in her secret hiding place at home. Unfortunately, her rendezvous was not a secret for long as in a few months her mother noticed her protruding belly.

"Enid, what you do? You pregnant? Your father gwine kill you! You throw away your life? Who did this to you?"

Her father overhears the conversation and walks in raging mad.

"Is who you sleeping with? You bring shame on our family?"

"I am sorry Papa."

He took off his belt and beat her mercilessly while she attempted to defend herself with her hands.

"Get out of my house and never come back you little whore. You are dead to us."

Even though her mother did not agree, she could not go against her husband's decision.

In tears, Enid grabs the jacket from its hiding place and makes her way to her favorite teacher's house. She was not easily consoled.

"My life is ruined Ms. Newsome. I don't know what to do. I am really desperate."

After Teacher Newsome made tea, Enid settled down.

"What about your grandmother? You should consider staying with her."

"No, Ms. Newsome, she is a minister and more judgmental than my father."

"Darling, you can stay here as long as you like but I think I have a solution. My sister and her husband desperately need a helper to take care of their four children. They both have full-time jobs. Are you interested?"

"Yes mam."

"Last week, their helper's husband was in a terrible car wreck and she returned home to take care of him".

So, the following day, Sunday, Teacher Newsome drove to Mandeville with Enid in tow. When they arrived, the children ran out to greet their auntie and immediately held hands with Enid. Mr. and Mrs. Marshall noticed how their children naturally took to Enid. The Marshalls did not care that she was pregnant; she was the one they could trust with the children and take care of their home. They were all treated to a wonderful Sunday dinner of brown-stew chicken with rice and peas. The highlight of the dinner though was the home-made, rum-raisin ice-cream that Mrs. Marshall mixed and Enid and the children helped turn the bucket with the rock salt and ice.

At dinner, the Marshalls offered Enid a live-in job. She would be paid each month to take care of the house as well as the washing, ironing. cooking and caring for the children. As Teacher Newsome departed, with good-bye hugs and kisses from the children, she assured Enid that everything would be alright. Enid indeed felt that she was in good hands. She liked the nice maid's quarters and felt at home. That night, while contemplating her parent's rejection, she exhaled, smiled contentedly, and fell asleep.

Come Monday morning, as soon as the sun was rising and the cock crowed, Enid made breakfast. She was particularly proud of the fried dumplings, fried eggs, bacon, and cornmeal porridge she prepared. Enid's mother had taught her well, but they didn't have amenities like electricity. Enid had to be taught what could go into the freezer. It was a minor crisis when she placed the bottle of water in the freezer and it exploded. Mrs. Marshall was very patient and just laughed at her innocent mistakes.

As the Marshalls left for work, Enid assured them that she would take care of everything including the three and one-year old who were left in her care. They sang, recited nursery rhymes, danced and played games. When they took their naps, Enid cleaned the house and made the beds. The children as well as Mr. and Mrs. Marshall loved the red pea soup she made each Saturday.

Mr. and Mrs. Marshall and the children fell in love with Enid. Mrs. Marshall was a teacher at Manchester High School and Mr. Marshall was the manager of the Nova Scotia Bank in Mandeville. The agreement was that Mr. Marshall would buy stock in his bank with half of Enid's salary each month. They were kind and considerate and always invited her to sit with the family for all their meals. Even so, Enid had to get up often to get food to the table of whatever the Marshalls needed. Mrs. Marshall took Enid to a doctor for pre-natal care. Unknown to Enid, Mrs. Marshall also drove the two hours to visit her sister as well as Enid's family to assure them that Enid was doing fine.

Again, unknown to Enid, Mrs. Marshall was updating Enid's mother about Enid's progress and Mrs. Stewart begged Mrs. Marshall to let them know about the birth of their grandchild. Mrs. Stewart insisted that Mr. Stewart reconcile with his daughter saying:

"Jesus Christ Manny, this is our one girl pickney we cannot just turn our backs on her."

Mr. Stewart softened and regretted how harshly he had treated his daughter.

On March 13, 1969, Enid's water broke. Mr. Marshall made the trip to bring Enid's parents to the hospital so they would be present for the birth of their grandchild. Enid was shocked when her parents walked in and they all hugged and cried. There was much relief, but Enid still did not appreciate it when her father said: "Sometimes, good things can come from the mistakes we make in life." She did not let him draw her tongue and give him a piece of her mind.

Everyone fell in love with the baby girl that Enid named Mavis Stewart Singer. The Marshalls became Mavis' godparents at her baptismal and committed to raise Mavis as one of their own. She had her own room in the main house. They also arranged for Mavis to spend holidays with her grandparents. They now had five children in the house, and it was one happy family. While Enid looked after the house and the children, Mavis not only excelled in school but could practice on the Marshall's piano along with the Marshall's youngest daughter. They entertained the family and friends singing beautiful songs together.

As Mavis grew into a young lady, Enid advised her to read and study, read and study, read and study like the Marshall's children who were not allowed to help with the household chores. Mavis was also a good athlete who practiced often and excelled in track,especially the 400 meters, and volleyball. Enid was active in her adopted church in Mandeville and when they attended, Mavis was called on to play the piano and lead the hymns.

When Mavis completed elementary school, she received a scholarship to Immaculate High School where she excelled academically, played the piano in the school orchestra and as a member of the relay team, won the 4x400 relay at CHAMPS, the national track meet for secondary schools. It made her mother, grandparents, and the Marshalls proud when Mavis graduated in 1989 as one of the top graduates receiving several ribbons and trophies for her achievements—-on and off the field.

As a result of the guidance counselor at Immaculate sending a dossier of her top ten students to several Canadian, American and English Colleges who were recruiting runners from Jamaica, Drake University in Des Moines, Iowa expressed an interest and after a telephone interview, offered her a full track scholarship. Mr. Marshall, acting like a proud Papa helped her obtain a Jamaican passport, an American student visa and booked her ticket. Mavis excitedly packed her bags and was ready to go. She made plans to arrive in Des Moines for the fall session in 1989.

The Marshalls took pains to school her about life in the United States. They taught her how to deal with the racism and prejudice she would encounter. Mr. Marshall advised her:

"Mavis, you are there to get an education. Do not be distracted. Focus on your goal. Don't be discouraged or take offense at every insult or rebuff. At the end of the day, everything is small stuff." The entire family was present for the send-off at the airport.

Mavis felt like she was on the precipice of a new adventure. When the plane took off and unexpectedly dropped in an air pocket, she let out an embarrassing scream. The rest of her flight to New York and her connecting flight to Des Moines was without trauma. This was her first time in the United States, so she wasn't shy about asking a lot of questions and people were generally helpful even though she had to repeat herself due to her Jamaican accent. A college representative met her at the Des Moines airport, welcomed her and helped her with her luggage. Mr. Marshall had warned her about the cold weather in Iowa but when she arrived at the end of August, the weather was the same as Jamaica.

In a few months, however, when a cold front came through, the temperature dropped below freezing. She couldn't catch her breath, her knees stiffened up and her fingers, ears and nose felt like they were about the drop off. She quickly understood that she was not in Jamaica anymore—jacket, hat, gloves, and boots were required.

Mavis quickly acclimated to her new circumstances. She not only excelled at track, it appeared that Immaculate High had prepared her well, so she received good grades and graduated in four years (1992) still complaining about Iowa winters. She was very popular and almost everyone was kind and considerate. Her girlfriends were forever asking her to show them Jamaican dance moves. With Mavis anchoring the team, Drake came in second in the 4x400 relays being beaten by a strong Jamaican team. She didn't feel too bad about it as the Jamaica team won as usual and she absolutely enjoyed visiting with fellow Jamaican girls.

Mavis graduated with honors and matriculated to law school at the University of Iowa in Iowa City. While there, she met another Jamaican, who was studying medicine. Mr. Errol McFarlane overheard the Jamaican accent while they waited in line to attend a concert and asked: "Do my ears deceive me or do I hear the voice of someone from Yard?" She smiled and reached out her hand: "I am Mavis Singer." Once they were introduced, the two Jamaicans on campus gravitated to each other. When they graduated, they both returned to Jamaica and obtained jobs—he as attending doctor at the University of the West Indies at Mona and she with the Law Firm of Stewart and McKenzie. Even though Mavis had passed the Bar exam in the United States, she was required to attend law school at the University of the West Indies for one year before she was eligible to join the Jamaica Bar.

To celebrate her passing the Jamaica Bar, Errol took her to the restaurant at the Terra Nova Hotel. He had arranged for his favorite waiter to serve them. He ordered for her and after the champagne and food arrived, the waiter lifted the silver covering to reveal a beautiful diamond ring. He immediately went to his knees and popped the question:

"Will you make me the happiest man alive and become my wife?" Although it was not entirely unexpected, it was still a thrill.

"Yes, yes, yes. I am all yours, now and forever." Mavis was overcome with joy. As they kissed, all the patrons for the evening applauded. Some even stopped by their table to congratulate them. They were all smiles.

They set the date for their wedding for June 19, 1994 but Errol insisted that they wouldn't invite any country people that could potentially embarrass them. He particularly did not want his parents to find out that her mother was a maid and that she didn't even know who her father was. She said: "No Errol, we cannot do this. My mother and grandparents would die if they were not invited to our wedding. We just cannot do this." But he insisted and she gave in to his demands.

When Mrs. Marshall saw Enid crying on the veranda, Mrs. Marshall said:

"So, what is it now? Why you crying?"

"Me belly bottom bun Mrs. Marshall. For all these years, I lived for her, working hard to send the pickney to school and now she getting married to a doctor and she does not want me to come to her wedding. She even tells me that I cannot ever visit her in town because I am just a country woman who speaks patois. She says she will send me money and visit me from time to time but her husband objects to me helping to raise their children. What a 'botheration' Mrs. Marshall."

"I don't believe it. She really going to turn her back on you after all you did for her. I don't believe it."

"It's not that she doesn't love me, you understand, I think she does. She is just ashamed of being a bastard. I cannot help it if I don't know who her father is. I never even met her husband or any of his family."

"Don't make excuses for her, Enid. She is an ungrateful wretch and why would any man want to marry a woman who disrespects her own mother? You think she can just turn her back on her mother? God does not like ugly. But Enid, Mr. Marshall and I have an important decision to make. She invited my husband to give her away and for our family to attend and pretend to be her family. I don't think we can do that in deference to you."

"No, Mrs. Marshall, I beg you to go. I want her to be happy even if I am upset at her decision. You must go. I insist. She will come around one day. Please go and enjoy yourselves."

So, with the Marshalls in attendance and Mr. Marshall giving away the bride, Mavis and Errol were married at the University of the West Indies Chapel, had a fancy reception at Terra Nova Hotel and honeymooned at the Half Moon Hotel in Mobay. After three years of marriage, they became the proud parents of two children.

It was not long before Dr. Errol McFarlane was having affairs with several nurses. When one of them became pregnant and he had to confess his infidelities, Mavis ordered him to leave and he moved out and to live with the woman who was having his third child.

As a lawyer, and single mother, Mavis was working overtime and was able to supervise her home. She discovered that her helper was giving both of her children rum to keep them calm and manageable. She immediately fired the helper, but then discovered that she and both children had the SARS virus in 2003 and could not work. She was in a bad place.

Mrs. Mavis McFarlane finally begged her mother to visit after their quarantine. Ms. Enid complied and when Ms. Enid drove up to Mavis's house in her BMW, she ran out to hug her mother. They were both in tears. "I am so sorry mommy. I was such a fool. You are the best mother in the world and I truly love you. Please forgive me."

"Mavis, you will always be my daughter and I will always carry you in my heart." As the Marshalls were now empty nesters, they agreed that Ms. Enid should move to town to help raise her grandchildren. So, Enid took up residence at her daughter's house in Kingston in 2004 being careful not to contract the SARS virus.

Mavis had to confess that Errol was not helping them financially. And due to some unwise investments in the Olint investment scheme, she was in trouble financially. Enid said not to worry as she was now a rich woman. The money Mr. Marshall had invested for her in Nova Scotia Bank for over thirty years paid off handsomely and neither she nor her family ever had to work again. She called it "Easy Street." Enid then took the blue jacket out of her suitcase and made a present of it to her daughter.

"This is your inheritance."

She then told the story of meeting her father that fateful day under the breadfruit tree.

Mavis smiled. "You are a bad woman and I am jealous."

AUTHOR'S NOTE

Adolescence is a time of significant growth and development inside the teenage brain. Because the prefrontal cortex is still developing, teenagers might rely on a part of the brain called the amygdala to make decisions and solve problems more than adults do. This might explain why teenagers' decisions are often more emotional than rational. Emerging science about brain development suggests that most people's brains do not reach full maturity until age 25. In "The Snoring Bandit," a young Glenroy aspires to become prosperous, but he makes an irrational decision that could have serious consequences.

The Snoring Bandit

Basil Kong

No history or map of Jamaica will include any reference to Woodside District, St. Elizabeth. The world may be ignorant of its existence but for those who know the place, it becomes part of their soul. Everyone here knows each other so well, they can point out who owns the many dogs, cows, goats, cats and even chickens that roam the community. Social friendliness prevails with a pledge to take care and pray for each other. Two hundred little wood and zinc houses dot the hillsides, and the people live in peace and tranquility.

Woodlanders' build their homes in remote hills to enjoy the stately panorama, but more importantly, to see approaching friends or foe in time to either run to greet them or go into hiding. They are remote from the troubles of the world that they occasionally read about in week-old copies of *The Gleaner*, the newspaper that villagers brought back from "Town."

Helping yourself to sugarcane, mangoes, naseberries, grapefruit, oranges, tangerines, plums and guineps from a neighbor's property was not considered a crime. All the "pickney dem," the children from the district, enjoyed this privilege including Glenroy, a precocious twelve-year-old who lived with his mother, grandmother and two brothers.

His father had migrated to England. When he was ten years old, Glenroy confessed to his grandmother that he was going to be very rich someday. "I am going to be somebody important," he declared. And so began his obsession with getting his hands on some money.

With a special request from his grandmother, the owners of the shop, Claudie and Myra MacDonald, hired Glenroy as the yard boy to tend to their small home garden. Granny was so pleased she hugged him and uttered her favorite catchphrase: "Can you imagine?"

They paid him a shilling a day. However, with his powerful ambition he had set his sights on much bigger things in life. He saw the lack of money as a great wall to overcome.

He would often observe his employers emptying the money till into a small leather 'grip' – a suitcase that they took to their nearby home after closing. Glenroy set his sights on stealing the grip. He concocted a plan to break into his employer's house and lay in wait for them to come home. He did not want to hurt anyone, just to grab the grip when Mass Claudie and Ms. Myra fell asleep and quietly make his escape. He reasoned that the McDonalds were so rich, they would not even miss that little bit of money, and it would give him a start on the road to prosperity.

One evening, as the sun was going down, Glenroy activated his plan. He slipped through the window into the bedroom and hid under the couple's bed. He laid quietly under the bed for several hours and daydreamed of being a "Big Man" with his own house and a horse. Soon he imagined he would become the envy of the entire community and have the adoration of girls all over town. The thought made him smile. He envisioned himself riding around the village on the back of a white horse wearing a wide-brimmed hat and waving to his admirers.

When the shopkeepers arrived home that fateful evening, they placed the grip conspicuously on their bureau, washed up, changed into their night clothes, and slid under the covers. A little while later when

Mass Claudie tried to cozy up to his wife, he heard snoring. He stiffened his forefinger and "jooked" his wife. "Myra, you fall asleep already? Me in the mood you know!"

She responded, "A no me a snore!"

"Not you?" Mass Claudie responded in shock.

Whereupon they stared at each other and realized that someone was snoring under their bed.

Poor Glenroy had fallen asleep and was now snoring loudly.

Mass Claudie jumped out of his bed and grabbed a broom from behind the door and repeatedly hit the intruder.

"Tief! Tief! Tief!" He yelled as loud as he could.

When Glenroy emerged from under the bed Miss Myra said: "Oh my God, is that you Glenroy? Mass Claudie could kill you, you brute." Mass Claudie then yelled out some bad words and aggressively ran Glenroy out of their house. The ruckus woke everyone in this sleepy village and Glenroy, suffering the agony of his lacerated conscience, ran away in disgrace.

He ran and didn't stop until he reached Tenancy Mountain. He had only the clothes on his back and felt extremely afraid. Fortunately, it was a full moon. Here was a 12-year-old boy barefoot in the bush all alone in the middle of the night. For the first time in his life, he had no one to talk to or harass. He reflected on Teacher Ferguson telling the class that other than mongoose and wild hogs, Jamaica had no dangerous animals, but every duppy story he ever heard came back to his mind. He told himself that when people died, they were just that – dead! They did not turn into duppies. They were not real, but in this situation, he was not so sure. He gathered up some leaves to make a bed and burst into tears. Every strange sound he heard startled him as he tried to catch a nap. The day before, he dreamed of being a hero but for now he only wanted to survive the night. He fully expected to be awakened by the District Constable, put in handcuffs, and lead off to prison. He was now an outlaw.

Glenroy's grandmother, who was worried and embarrassed begged the MacDonalds to forgive him. Because she enjoyed a good relationship with them, they agreed to let it go as nothing was stolen.

Glenroy didn't know that the McDonalds were not going to press charges, so he was terrified to return home. He decided to "hide a bush"—take his chances and stay in the woods—washing in a pond and surviving by eating fruits and berries. It was mango season, so he had no trouble keeping his belly full of these succulent fruits.

In his wanderings for two days, he 'bucked upon' the man they called "Little Man" tending to his ganja plants beside a pond. Glenroy, feeling compelled to have human contact, yelled out, "Wha gwaan sah?"

Not expecting anyone, Little Man was startled and looked around to where the voice came from and found Glenroy up a tree. "Hey man, everybody talking about you! How you do?"

"Me getting along."

After helping to weed around the fifty or so ganja plants, Little Man offered him a cartwheel dumpling with fried pork, served on a coco leaf, as well as some hard dough bread and lemonade made with sour oranges and wet sugar. Little Man then took out a spliff, and they took turns smoking and getting high.

"That's some good ganja you have Little Man."

As their chance encounter wound down, he asked Little Man for some matches so he could make a fire. The meeting reminded Glenroy of home, and he felt sad but returned to the bush and asked Little Man not to tell anyone where he was. But of course, this was news Little Man found impossible to keep to himself.

On the third day of his isolation, sitting on a limb high in a tree eating a mango, he heard his brothers calling out his name. Glenroy was thrilled to hear his brothers' voices but was overcome by his urge to play a trick on them. As his brothers approached the tree, they noticed the freshly discarded mango skins and seeds and decided that Glenroy must be nearby.

Glenroy jumped from the mango tree with a blood curdling yell. His brothers jumped back but quickly recognized him. Overcome with joy, they hugged and sat down to talk.

They informed him that his crime was forgiven and that his mother and grandmother were anxious to have him back home. They told him that no one was angry, but everyone was definitely laughing about the incident.

Hearing this news, he meekly accompanied his brothers out of the woods and back home. He was expecting the worst, but to his surprise, his brothers as well as his mother were glad to see him back home. It reminded him of the story in the Bible about the 'Prodigal Son'.

In her joy, his granny hugged him as she never did before. While it was not the fatted calf, he was treated to curry chicken and rice as well as a proper bath. Ms. Ida, his mother was particularly glad that he was safe. Her family was together again. Glenroy promised them that he would get rich the right way.

Later, whenever they recalled this story they all had a good laugh. When granny was finished laughing, she turned to her family and said: "Can you imagine?"

AUTHOR'S NOTE

In the early 1900s, Jamaicans went to Panama to find work when the US took over the building of the canal. Many eventually settled there and as a result, there is a thriving enclave of Jamaican culture on the isthmus. You can find people there who speak like a Jamaican but have never ever set foot on Jamaican soil, yet, they enjoy the same food and customs as the islanders do.

In "The Man from Boca," the hero connects with his Jamaican roots after a life at sea when he marries Muriel, a Jamaican he meets in New York.

The Man from Boca

Glen Laman

Friday

As the Delta Airlines flight from Atlanta approached Sangster's International Airport in Montego Bay, Muriel looked out her window at the emerald sea below and teared up as the island shoreline came into view. The sight of sand and sea brought back many memories and a flood of emotions. She touched her son Peter's arm and pointed to the window.

"My island in the sun!" she exclaimed excitedly.

Prior to the trip, she had done a lot of shopping and bought numerous gifts for her brothers and sisters who still lived on the island. All the bags were overweight, but she was happy to pay the excess baggage fees.

After disembarking, she and Peter followed the lines towards immigration and customs. The immigration agent stamped their passports and waved them on. They collected their luggage: several large suitcases and a box from the carousel.

Muriel and Peter joined the green line at customs with a large sign that read, "Nothing to Declare."

As they approached the customs agent Peter whispered to his mother.

"Remember, if they ask what you have just tell them some personal effects."

"What if "them" search everything?"

"Just relax, everything will be okay," Peter reassured her.

Ahead of them, the female agent was searching the suitcases of a middle-aged female passenger. To the dismay of the passenger, they found ten pairs of shoes and numerous pocketbooks.

"Are these for resale?" the agent asked.

"No man, me just a stock up for me nuh know when me can shop again," replies the passenger.

"I'm sorry miss but you will have to join the next line and pay duty," responds the agent.

At the sight of this, Muriel started to shake and laments.

"Bwoy dem rough with the people them sah!"

"Don't worry mother, she had stuff to sell. You don't have twenty pairs of shoes or anything like that," Peter reassured her.

The female passenger packs up her merchandise and goes to pay the customs duty. The agent signals for Muriel and Peter to approach. Peter hoists the big suitcases onto the platform. The agent looks at Muriel and asks, "What do you have in that handbag?"

Muriel trembles a little then exclaims, "Is just my husband's ashes."

Peter looks at his mother with his mouth wide-open, shakes his head, and throws his arms wide open.

"I'm sorry but you will need a certificate from the board of health," says the agent in a stern voice.

"We just going throw the ashes in the sea, you know, man," says Peter imitating a Jamaican accent.

"It nuh matter. You still have to get authorization to bring it onto the island," retorts the agent.

"Okay. Where do I go to get that?" asks Muriel.

"Well, they are closed today Friday. Nothing can be done before Monday. You must first go to the St. James Parish Council and pay for a permit, you then take that receipt to the Board of Health and they will issue a certificate. Once you get a certificate from the board of health, bring the certificate back here to customs to claim the ashes," explained the agent.

"What! But we are staying all the way in St. Elizabeth. I will have to travel back to Montego Bay. Is there nothing else you can do?

"I am sorry, but you have to get the permits before you can get the ashes ma'am."

Muriel is annoyed by this aggravating development but is determined to have a good trip and show her son some of the island's many offerings.

Sunday

Since they arrived in St. Elizabeth, many family and friends have been stopping by to see them and express condolences. Muriel decides to show Peter around the parish which was known as the bread basket of Jamaica, because of its many farm products. Today they are on their way to nearby Lover's Leap, a steep cliff with an exhilarating and spectacular view where the Santa Cruz mountains meet the Caribbean Sea. According to legend, Mizzy and Tunki were two slaves from a nearby plantation, in the 18th century, who chose to leap to their death rather than be separated when their master tried to sell Tunki to another plantation.

As they tour the observation deck and visit the adjoining lighthouse which is the highest in the Western Hemisphere, memories of the many visits she and her late husband, Pappy, made to this beautiful spot flood Muriel's thoughts. They would often have a drink in the bar while enjoying the view. What a love they shared! It was a love "which many waters could not quench," as the song goes.

The day before they had visited Treasure Beach to unwind and take their minds off the unexpected drama at the airport. The sea breeze had a calming effect on them as they basked in the tropical sun.

Muriel's thoughts, despite her efforts, now turned again to Pappy's ashes.

She was still reeling from the encounter with the customs agent. Why did she blurt out that she had the ashes when she had planned otherwise? Her mind was a mess.

"What am I going to do with the ashes?" She had asked before booking the flight. After various calls and enquiries with no answer, she had simply placed the urn with the ashes in her handbag.

She had wanted so much for his final wishes to go off smoothly.

Pappy was born and raised in the Panama Canal Zone. His parents, both Jamaicans, moved there to find work in the early part of the 20th century building the canal. The French started building the Panama Canal, but the difficulty of cutting through mountains plus thousands of deaths from malaria and yellow fever forced them to abandon the project. The United States then assumed control and completed it in 1914. Thousands of Caribbean workers, including Jamaicans, signed up for this enormous project.

Life was not easy for the Jamaicans in the Canal Zone, a US territory that was five miles wide on either side along the length of the 50-mile canal. The administration classified them as "silver roll" workers who received lesser pay, benefits, and accommodations than the "gold roll" workers from the US did. Nevertheless, they made a life and many of their descendants are there to this day.

Pappy showed athletic prowess and as a young man earned the nickname, "El Caballo," the great horse. He represented Panama in the fourth Central American and Caribbean Games earning a gold medal for the relays. Although good at sports, he would end up working at sea most of his life.

He started as a dishwasher on a passenger ship. He gradually worked his way up the ladder and when he retired from the shipping line, he was an executive chef.

He showed up at Muriel's apartment one evening accompanied by her sister with whom he had worked with on the Grace Lines. He was a friend of her sister's husband.

"I am your man from Boca," he said with a smile.

"Where on earth is Boca?" she asked.

"Panama. It's the town where I was born and raised."

"I have an uncle who went to Panama. I think he lived in Colon," she explained.

Muriel was not feeling well that first evening when they met, but the handsome stranger lifted her spirits. She was also just getting over a breakup and wanted nothing to do with men. But he seemed different than all the men she had ever known.

"All my life I have been waiting to meet someone like you," he said charmingly.

"Get out of here! You probably have a girl in every port," she answered with a big laugh.

"Actually, I have been married and divorced and have learned a lot. So, whoever gets me now is getting a big prize," he chuckled. "I just retired from the sailing ships and looking forward to settling down with somebody just like you."

"Well keep looking. I have had it with men."

"Don't say that. You haven't had it with me and I just know the best is yet to come for you."

Somehow, they kept running into each other. Her sister's birthday party. Family gatherings. He was there. She soon realized he was an excellent cook. In addition, he was thoughtful, kind, and considerate. And, just like that a whirlwind romance ensued.

Within a few months, they got married and bought a house in Queens. It was a second marriage for both, and this helped them to appreciate what they had even more. It was not long before she was pregnant with their son Peter.

Pappy loved entertaining and everyone delighted in his recipes. Each meal was a masterpiece. "Presentation is everything, your eyes will see the food before you eat, so it must be pleasing to the eye," was a constant refrain of his. Muriel had so many wonderful memories of him.

Peter was enjoying himself. His first visit to the island when he was only five did not go so well. The rural landscape and farming life did not impress him. There was no place to get hamburgers and fries and so he wanted to go home. While his parents would make an annual trek to the island, he had stayed away.

This time he was paying attention to everything and seeing them with fresh eyes. He marveled at the cows, goats, and chickens that seemed to wander freely across the land, unperturbed by the goings on. He admired the plants, the bananas and coconuts, orange trees, the mango and ackee trees. Now he could appreciate why his father was so fond of coming to this land so much.

His father had a wonderful sense of humor; he saw the funny side of everything and told him many stories of his life at sea. There was the time on a voyage to Asia his crewmates rushed to the side of the ship when the captain announced that they were crossing the International Date Line. Only then did they realize that it was an imaginary line.

Once when his father visited Turkey, a group from the ship went to the Black Sea wanting to see if the water was indeed black. They were very disappointed that it was no different from any other sea.

Pappy had packed so much into his life. He had worked on merchant ships during World War II carrying supplies across the oceans. He was always aware that at any time enemy destroyers, aircraft or German submarines known as U-boats could attack and sink them. Years later, he would receive a commendation for service in the Merchant Marine.

Monday

After a three-hour drive from Top Hill, Muriel and Peter are back in Montego Bay early in the morning at the Parish Council to pay for the permit for the ashes. Her brother-in-law Leroy is acting as their chauffeur for the trip. They arrive at the St. James Parish Council office to find a long line of people waiting to get in.

'Wow, I didn't think it would be this busy," exclaimed Peter.

"But the line not moving. Why don't you go up front and see what's going on?" Muriel suggests.

Peter makes his way to the front door of the building. He chats with a security guard and then comes back to his mother.

"It's a power failure. The building has no electricity. Elevators not working," he explains.

"Welcome to the Third World," adds a woman waiting in line.

"They must think we have nothing to do but waste time in a long line," chimes in another woman.

"Half a day's work for half a day's pay," says a man in a "Jamaica No Problem" t-shirt.

"Is anyone up there? We come all the way from country this morning and we not going back to come again," Muriel explains to the security guard.

"Yes, people upstairs but the elevator no working," says the guard.

"Well, we don't mind using the stairs. Which floor to get a permit for the Board of Health," asks Muriel.

"Third floor. But hold onto the rails, it dark, dark," says the security guard.

"Muriel and Peter head towards the stairs. The security guard yells up the stairs,

"Two people coming!"

A man on the third floor is waving a flashlight to illuminate the stairway for them. They grab the rails and slowly work their way up to the third floor. When they get to the office, they discover people are at work using the light coming through the windows. They explain that they need a permit for the ashes and after making a payment, the clerk issues them one. She instructs them to take the permit to the Board of Health where they will be issued a health certificate.

They get back in the car and head towards the Cornwall Regional Hospital where the offices of the Board of health are located.

"What a trial over a few ashes," Muriel says to herself. Her Pappy would be annoyed at all the trouble just to dispose of his ashes in the sea. He was such an organized person. He was neatness personified. He always had his affairs lined up in order.

His friends always joked that he was the only person who could cook a six-course meal in a tuxedo and still look impeccable afterwards. Everything was so well prepared and laid out ahead of time; he washed his pots and pans while he cooked so that by the time he was finished cooking there was no washing up to be done.

Now his final request of scattering his ashes in the Jamaican waters as a nod to his life at sea. It was turning out to be a mess.

He always said that the sea had a kind of magic. "It is a tonic for the wear and tear of life." He found it calming and restorative. It was only fitting that he wanted to make his final voyage in the waters off the land he loved.

When they arrived at the Board of Health office, the waiting room is empty. They explain their mission to the secretary.

She tells them there is no one in the office to sign off on the permit required. She explains that the two doctors who are authorized to do it are not there today.

"But we have come so far," wails Muriel. "So much fuss over some ashes. We have to get that permit today."

"Please have a seat ma'am. Let me make a few calls to see if anyone else can assist," the secretary says trying to help.

An hour later, there is still no resolution. Muriel is frustrated. The secretary is working the phones to find a solution. Peter nervously starts to walk the hallways of the hospital.

He knew everything would eventually be sorted out but it was frustrating. His father would not be pleased with all the drama over his ashes. Why did his mother have to be so honest. How would his father react to this hiccup now?

He recalled that Pappy's first visit to the US did not go well. It was a voyage that took him to the Port of Baltimore, Maryland. He and another crew member from Panama collected their pay envelopes and went to a bank to change some of the large bills they had been given. The bank personnel were not welcoming, but they grudgingly changed the money.

Before they could exit the bank, police officers with guns drawn surrounded them, and placed them in handcuffs. The bank personnel had reported them as suspicious black men with a lot of cash. Fortunately, a call to the ship's captain confirmed where the money came from and they were immediately released.

Pappy had certainly come a long way. He was not one to hold grudges and always told that story as if it were a comedy. A true Jamaican, he knew how to "take bad things make laugh." He could make a sad story into a comedy.

Suddenly, Peter's thoughts are interrupted by the secretary dashing down the hallway. She had located someone who could sign the certificate.

"Thank you, Jesus!" exclaimed Muriel.

"We can't thank you enough," said Peter. "Can we give you a tip? You have saved us a lot of grief."

"Oh no," said the secretary. "We not allowed to accept any gifts."

Wednesday

It was a beautiful morning in Alligator Pond, a fishing village some thirty minutes' drive from where Muriel and Peter were staying. There is a big ship anchored not too far from the coast. The sea is calm, and a gentle wind is blowing. A perfect day to take Pappy's ashes out to sea. Muriel has a bouquet of flowers and Peter has the urn with the ashes. They are ready to head out with Roland who owns and operates the boat they will use.

Muriel begins to tear up as Roland guides her onto the boat. Peter carefully cradles the urn and balances himself as the wind picks up. As the boat heads out to sea, Muriel gets more emotional.

The boat comes to a stop and Roland shuts off the engine. The shoreline in the distance is gleaming in the morning sun. The Don Figueroa Mountains are in the background and as they look up, they can see the alligator shape that gave the beach its name.

Peter touches his mother's hand, "Mother do you want to sing a song?" She nods and they start singing Bob Marley's *Three Little Birds,* as Peter stands up in the boat and reaches for the urn.

"This is the moment," he says, as he uncovers the urn and scatters the ashes overboard.

"Goodbye, Pappy," says Muriel as she wipes tears from her eyes.

"Rest in Peace," says Peter as he covers the urn and sits down.

Roland starts the engine, and they head for shore. To their left, the big ship is now in motion. It turns and now heads out into the ocean. They pass the ship silently and wave to no one in particular.

"Wow, it didn't take long for Pappy to find another ship headed to the deep blue sea," exclaims Peter.

"I like how they were waiting for us to scatter his ashes before casting off."

"Yes," says Muriel, "looks like it was all pre-arranged."

"Bon Voyage," says Peter.

AUTHOR'S NOTE

Tourism is a staple industry in Jamaica. As a result, there are many options for visitors to stay on the island, from the big and bland all-inclusives to exclusive, luxury hotels or private, seaside cottages.

Many Jamaicans dream of owning a small hotel or bed and breakfast. One reason is you can be your own boss plus the added incentive of earning coveted foreign exchange which can insulate you from fluctuations in the local currency. Another positive is meeting people from all over the globe, many of whom can become lifelong friends. With the advent of Airbnb, there has been an incredible rise in the popularity of boutique bed and breakfasts. The challenges include keeping demanding tourists happy and holding on to staff. It is an open secret that many people travel to the island not just for sun and sea but also in search of love.

Bed & Breakfast Blues

Glen Laman

Beverly Jones was in her office making a few calls. Her small bed and breakfast in Ocho Rios had been operating at full capacity all winter. An unusually harsh winter had sent snowbirds from all over Europe, the United States and Canada and now she was looking forward to visitors from the Land of the Rising Sun - a party of five from Japan.

She was about to dial another number when a guest walked in with a complaint.

"I think I lost my bag on the Dunn's River tour yesterday."

"I'm sorry to hear that Mrs. Harper. I will check with the driver. What color was it?"

"It's yellow and blue with red handles."

"Okay. I will make a few inquiries and let you know what I find."

In her twenty years in the business nothing surprised Beverly anymore. She had seen her share of broken pipes and overflowing toilets. She had spent hours waiting in emergency rooms when careless tourists hurt themselves. Despite the repeated warnings to avoid over exposure to the hot sun, there were always sunburn cases. One night she had to wheel a drunken guest to his room on a luggage cart as he was too inebriated to walk. Then you had the guests who wanted to hoodwink you so they can get free drinks, meals, or even free stays. One guest wanted a refund when it rained because his travel agent had assured him that there was only sunshine in Jamaica all year round.

The biggest scare was when a German family called to say their ten-year-old daughter was missing in Ocho Rios. Beverly's heart was racing as she tried to calm the mother down. After questioning the mother, she jumped in her car and raced back to town, only a few minutes away. After retracing their steps, little Heidi was found calmly sitting in a stall in the crafts market. A female vendor was braiding her hair. Oh happy day! What a relief that was!

Beverly smiled as she remembered the very conservative Juliet from Michigan who left her husband every year to spend weeks with her Jamaican lover. "Unbelievable," she thought. "that woman would not even look at a black man when she is in America." And then there was Karen who visited annually and had a thing for fishermen. Every year she brought random fishermen into her room although she had been warned that it was not wise to pick up complete strangers.

The trophy for most unbelievable guest would have to go to "Janet the bride," who told everyone she was the bride of Jesus. Her wardrobe contained only wedding dresses. She wore a wedding dress to breakfast, on tours, to the beach and even when she went shopping. She exhausted the supply of paper towels as she had to spread them out before taking each step because she insisted her feet could not touch the ground.

The airport bus pulled into the driveway. The driver began to unload luggage as five weary travelers stepped from the air-conditioned bus into the tropical sun.

Beverly walked out to greet them.

"Welcome to the Coconut Tree Bed and Breakfast. We have been expecting you. You must be the Takagis."

Mr. and Mrs. Takagi, their two grown daughters, Sakura and Yua along with Mrs. Takagi's sister Niko smiled and bowed slightly.

She hands them an information packet containing the keys to their rooms.

"Domo Arigato Gazimas. Thank you very much."

"You're welcome. Please follow me to your rooms. Your luggage will be delivered shortly."

After the Takagis are settled in, Beverly heads back to her office when an employee intercepts her.

"Miss Beverly, we have a big problem."

"What is it now Rosey?"

"We don't have enough chicken for dinner today, Miss."

"What you mean, Ronald didn't order any supplies for the kitchen?"

"No Miss. Him mind gone abroad. Ever since dat England woman fall in love with him, him can't focus."

"Oh Lawd!"

"Yes Miss, him just a daydream. Him just waiting on some documents she sending for him."

"Thank you Rosey. Let me call the market and see what I can do."

As Rosey leaves, a handsome young man walks in.

"Good morning, I am looking for an employee, Ann-Marie."

"Oh, she is no longer working here, sir."

"Do you know where I can find her, Miss?"

"She got married to a former guest and migrated to America," explains Beverly.

"You joking with me, right?"

"No man. Is a long story, but a man, his mother and his girlfriend came here on vacation over one year ago."

Beverly relates the story of how Ann-Marie got married.

She was working in the front office when Richard, his mother Martha and girlfriend Helen stayed here for a week. They had a great time and Ann-Marie interacted with them often and took care of their every need. She especially connected with Richard's mother, Martha. One day she remarked to her son, "You see that girl at the front desk; that is the woman you should be marrying instead of that crazy girlfriend of yours."

Richard laughed it off and they departed the island after a wonderful vacation. It was not long after that Richard started calling the office regularly to speak to Ann-Marie. Six months later, he came back to Jamaica. After a whirlwind romance, he proposed, they were married, and he took her with him back to America.

"I keep losing my staff to foreigners," lamented Beverly.

"So sorry," replies the young man.

"It's usually the men I lose. I have trouble keeping the cooks. Once a man can cook, he becomes especially attractive to many women. One time, three of them had eyes for the same cook. He could pick, choose, and refuse. He still calls us from Chicago from time to time."

"Well, I am very sorry I never acted sooner."

"Can you cook? You see that cook out there, he is also leaving soon to get married."

"I am not good at cooking, but I'm a good waiter. I am working over at the Moonlight Terrace Hotel, but if your cook wants to train me, I'm a fast learner. I am not interested in no foreign women because I don't like cold weather."

"That's nice. Leave your contact information with me in case something comes up."

"My name is Mervin. You can always find me at the Moonlight Terrace, but I'll leave my number as well."

They say goodbye and Mervin drives off.

That evening, the Takagis are in the outdoor dining area for their first dinner on the island. The waiter approaches and introduces himself as Roland.

Roland quickly learns that Sakura and Yua are the only ones in the family who speak English comfortably. They live in Itsunomiya, a small city about an hour's drive from Tokyo. They are big fans of Reggae and Dancehall music. And they love all things Jamaican. Sakura is a purchasing manager for an electronics firm while Yua is in her last year of college and studying chemistry.

After dinner, the older Takagis return to their rooms and Roland offers to give the young women a tour of the property. They gladly accept and join him in inspecting the beautiful gardens and tropical plants that adorn the bed and breakfast. They are impressed by his good manners and charming personality. He is quite handsome and has an outstanding physique due to the exercise program he conducts on the beach each morning.

They ask him about his family. He explains that he is from a town in the hills of St. Ann called Alderton. It is very small but is only a few miles from where Bob Marley was born. They are excited to hear this and want to know if he knows any of Bob's family. He tells them no; the family left the area a long time ago.

He compliments them on their names. They explain that Sakura means "cherry blossoms" and Yua means "binding love and affection."

For the next two weeks, Roland sees Sakura and Yua almost every morning at exercise before they join their parents and aunt for the tour of the day. Whenever they show up for dinner, he is their waiter of choice.

In their first week they visit Dunn's River Falls, Fern Gully, Bob Marley Museum in Kingston, and his birthplace in Nine Miles. During the second week they visit a Rastafari village, went rafting down a river, horseback riding in the sea and took a day trip to Negril's Seven Mile Beach.

Beverly could not help but notice that the young women were enthralled by her employee, Roland. They could hardly contain their excitement whenever they saw him. "Staff turnover was such a big issue, but what to do?" She thought to herself. "Such is the life of a Jamaican innkeeper."

Roland has also sensed that something was developing between him and the two Japanese women. Yua is very smart, and will no doubt be very successful at whatever she does in life. However, he is more attracted to Sakura as he feels more relaxed in her company and is attracted to her quiet dignity. He had met Derrick a Jamaican who had moved to Japan years ago after marrying a Japanese visitor. He was on vacation with his wife and son who was a rising track star in Japan. Derrick had spoken glowingly about his life in Japan and how much he admired the culture. Roland wondered of this could also happen to him.

The Takagis had been wonderful guests and tonight was their last dinner in Jamaica before flying to Tokyo. It had been a pleasure having them. They never complained and were always gracious. "Lord, let me have more guests like these."

They are all smiles as Beverly approaches their table. Roland had already taken their order and gone to the kitchen. Yua breaks the news," Sakura is going to marry Roland."

"What your parents think?" Asks Beverly.

"Our father thinks it is too soon. She hardly knows him," explains Yua. "I love him too, but he only has eyes for Sakura."

"I always wanted to marry a Jamaican," says Sakura. "And Roland is kind and good looking. He knows how to treat a woman. He has many of the qualities I am looking for in a husband. I feel we have a real connection."

"Okay my dear, but you will have to make another trip to marry him," explains Beverly.

"Don't worry. He promised he would wait for me."

"If there is anything I can do to help just let me know," volunteers Beverly.

Beverly thinks to herself, "I can see the handwriting on the wall. Sakura will be back in a few months for the wedding, and I will have to find a new employee. I am not excited about that as Roland has been a good worker, but I am happy that he has found love."

Beverly had added wedding packages to her offerings when she realized that her employees were becoming clients as they got married. It was always such a beautiful time at the bed and breakfast when love was in bloom.

A few months later she gets a reservation for twenty rooms from Japan. She picks up the phone and dials. "Moonlight Terrace? Can I please speak with Mervin?"

AUTHOR'S NOTE

There was a time when the housing landscape in Jamaica was replete with unfinished houses. These were not abandoned structures. Jamaicans with limited funds often built what they could afford. They planned to add on more rooms as funds became available. They would occupy one or two completed rooms with the rest of the structure under construction. This situation would last, not for months, but sometimes decades. In "A House for Mattie," we are given a look at some of her struggles in her quest and can share her joy when her dream is realized.

A House for Mattie

Glen Laman

It is market day and another beautiful day in the Garden Parish of St. Ann. Several white clouds drifted easily across the azure sky in the village of Silver Grove, some 10 miles from the north coast almost 2,000 feet above sea level.

Not far from Mattie's gate, farmers haul produce to market on donkeys and dray carts pulled by mules on the unpaved gravel road. Inside her gate, on her one-acre sloping property, workers lay cinder blocks for a new house.

In her yard, a cackling hen announces that she had just laid an egg. Two goats snack on the succulent multi-colored leaves of a croton plant. Mattie hangs freshly washed clothes to dry on the clothesline that stretched from her old house to a large mango tree in the yard. A small black and white dog barks at the passing donkeys and mules while workers mix and pour concrete for the foundation of her house.

Mattie's outdoor kitchen had collapsed years ago. She had given up cooking by firewood so she now uses a small kerosene tabletop stove. The outdoor toilet, a latrine, was a short walk down and away from the old house. Water was stored in several recycled oil drums beside the old house. She had no electricity, and lighting was provided by kerosene lamps.

Mattie picks up a shirt from her basket to hang on the line. "Simeon, go see if you can find the egg. One of the fowl dem just lay. Look under the cellar first. You know how dem love to hide the egg dem from we."

"Yes Grams," replied the skinny little boy.

"If you see Molly in the back, tell her I need her to run to Mr. Cigar shop and buy some flour and rice for dinner."

"She gone over Aunt Sissy house to play, Grams," replied Simeon.

"Well, after you find the egg, go tell her to come home."

Suddenly, there is a huge commotion at the front gate. Two men in red shirts are blocking the workmen from entering the worksite.

"What your problem? You nuh see we just trying to work here," exclaimed one of the workmen.

"Stop to rahtid. Stop!! We not allowing this construction. This a fe wi land this," shout the men in the red shirts.

"Miss Mattie beg you come talk to them man yah."

Mattie rushes over to the gate.

"What the backside unoo a do a me gate. Nuh make me gwaan bad you hear," says Mattie in a loud voice.

The redshirted men stand their ground and are blocking the men from moving bags of cement from a van to the house. They hold long sticks in a menacing manner.

A crowd quickly gathers at Mattie's gate. A man on a bicycle dismounts and tries to get around the crowd. Mattie recognizes the man and approaches him. "Missa Joe beg you go get the police. Dem man yah a cause trouble."

"Okay Miss Mattie. Me soon come." Missa Joe rides off on his bicycle.

Mattie is shaking and her heart is beating rapidly wondering how could this embarrassing situation come about? This new house is to replace the existing wattle and daub house, which her family had owned going back into the 1800s for many years. Her mother had lived and died in the old house. Her three children and three grandchildren were also born there, but everything is now falling apart. Whenever it rains, the thatched roof would leak. The walls are worn thin in places and she is afraid that if nothing is done soon, they would be sleeping outdoors.

Her firstborn son, Dwight, had gone to America on farm work and is sending money back. Simone her daughter and her three children live with her as did her other son Carl who is learning to be a mechanic. Mattie had been saving all her life for this house but the money from her banana and coffee sales are barely enough to keep food on the table. Occasionally, she would sell her chickens, pigs, or goats and sometimes even eggs to raise cash.

This part of the parish is very fertile. Simone and Carl are always busy planting and helping her with the crops. Anything they plant would grow easily and her one-acre plot is now full of fruit trees of every kind: oranges, tangerines, otaheite apples, guava, coffee, cocoa, naseberry, june plum, star apple, custard apple, coconut, tamarind, avocado (pears), papaya, you name it—it grew on her property.

Laying the foundation of her new house is a longtime dream come true. She is beginning to feel, at last, that her lifelong struggles are coming to an end. Mattie had met disappointment early in life when the father of her children abandoned her for another woman. Neighbors had told her that he suddenly found religion and married his new lover. Some say he married her because she is lighter-skinned than Mattie who has a very black complexion. Mattie, however, pressed on and raised her children by herself. And with Dwight now in a position to help make her dream of a new home come true, she could see the light at the end of her long tunnel.

The police arrive and interrupt her reverie. They instruct the red shirt men to cease and desist. The red shirt men walk away angrily shouting, "It not over yet. We nah go way." This brought a temporary relief to Mattie, but she was not at ease. What is she going to do about these men?

She had heard that her father was involved in many sexual liaisons with several women in the village. It wouldn't surprise her if the red shirt men were indeed his sons. She wonders if there were several more to come out of the woodwork and lay claim to the property.

A month later, all the walls of the house in place, plumbing work is underway and the materials for the roof are in the driveway. The plan is to finish two rooms with the money she is saving so that she and her children will have a place to live. Slowly but surely, as more money comes in, she will continue to add other rooms, and eventually, the whole house will be completed. The workers are wiring the house for electricity and she plans to build a water storage tank. However, that will also have to wait.

Like wildfire, the story of the work-stopping commotion in front of her house this morning spreads throughout the community. It is the most excitement the town has had in years since Errol Parker stole Ricky Jones' goat.

The villagers fan the incident with more rumors, speculation, and misinformation. "Me did hear say Mattie almost have heart attack when it happen," says one woman to another.

"You mean she might have to share up dat property with the man dem. Where them come from?"

"A Moneague them born, but them just move here few months ago."

"Mattie father did a sow some wild oats all over the place, eh?"

"Possession is nine tenths of the law though. Me no think dem have any claim."

"Me wonder if her father did leave any will?"

Two months later, Mattie officially moves into her half-finished house. Two bedrooms are usable as is the kitchen. Her bed is made up with the 'good' sheets that she barely uses. The kitchen is nice and spacious replete with the new propane gas stove from America which she was happy to receive from her son in America. No more kerosene fumes!

"God bless America!" she exclaimed as she lit the first flame under the pot of coffee in celebration of her new stove.

Mattie sips her coffee and puts up her feet on the new hassock. Feeling content, she begins to reminisce about her son Dwight. He was a bright boy but was always in trouble at school. He talked back to the teacher and he was often disruptive in class and never interested in schoolwork. Once when a teacher tried to discipline him with a leather belt, he grabbed the belt out of the teacher's hand. She smiles and shakes her head at the memory. He was offered a half scholarship to a high school in Kingston but I could not afford it. When they approached his father, he offered no assistance. Dwight simply left school when his primary school education was over. He never seemed disappointed as he was more mechanically inclined and preferred working on cars than doing homework.

To make money and stay busy, Dwight did odd jobs fixing cars and helping people with repairs around their homes. This source of income was sporadic and left him in a 'feast or famine' existence. One day a friend told him that they were recruiting workers for farms in Florida. He applied, although he had no experience farming and did not like farm work. To his surprise, he was accepted and he passed the medical tests with flying colors.

Farm work did not agree with Dwight. After a couple of months, he defected from the farm program and found his way to New York.

When Mattie had started noticing that her old house was falling apart, a sense of fear and anxiety came over her. And every day she would notice further evidence of deterioration. When Dwight started to send money from America, she was so relieved and always sang his praises to friends and family. She did not hear from him for months and was worried sick that some disaster had overtaken him. Luckily, Dwight managed to send word with someone that he would write soon. Having gone AWOL from the farm program he had to keep a low profile until he could legalize his status in America.

In New York, once his legal issues were resolved, Dwight put his mechanical skills to work and soon had his own thriving foreign car repair business. This was how he was able to send some money to his mother every month. Mattie was so proud of him.

Mattie grows pensive as she reflects on the host of problems she had to get where she is now. The first contractor she hired disappeared with her money after doing very little work. One supplier demanded payment of the full invoice even though she had made a deposit of 50%. It was his word against hers as the receipt he gave her did not show the correct balance. One morning she would discover that thieves had raided the work site and made off with bags of cement and rods of steel.

"You think it easy," Mattie spoke out loud. "But I give thanks." She raises her hand above her head in supplication to the Lord.

Mattie smiles as she remembers the small feast she put on to celebrate her new home. There were several temporary wood fireplaces set up in her yard with large pots cooking bananas, dumplings, and yellow yam. Rice was cooking in large black pots with three legs. Two wide oversized Dutch pots were cooking curried goat. Several women helped with cooking and serving. Her daughter, Joanie, was mixing a large container of "wash," a version of lemonade made with Seville orange and dark sugar. Someone had brought a load of jelly coconuts on a donkey drawn dray and a young man was busy cutting then open with a machete.

Outside the house, under a mango tree, several men were drinking jelly coconuts while one man with a bottle of white rum was busy pouring rum into their coconuts. The servers start dishing out curried goat and rice. People grabbed their plates and utensils as a line formed.

Mattie showed off her modern house with indoor plumbing and kitchen to several women.

A few months later, the two red shirt men who had laid claim to her property have disappeared. She had sought advice from the local school principal. He initiated a   review of the court records which revealed that the house belonged to her mother and not her father. It was her mother who had paid the taxes year after year and eventually had the title transferred to her name. The red shirt men had no case. What a day of rejoicing that was! The principal asked the two men to come and see him. When they did, he explained the situation and asked them to apologize to Mattie. They did and everyone shook hands and vowed to help each other as they were siblings.

Mattie sips the last of her coffee and gazes out her kitchen window while a hen cackles to announce the arrival of another egg. Outside, a lone goat is feeding on the leaves of the croton plant.

AUTHOR'S NOTE

There used to be a poppy show man in every town who stood out with his outlandish costumes and eccentric behavior. He is the center of attention or makes a spectacle of himself. He is admired by some and laughed at by others, but he will attract the attention of everyone. He is always the "bride at every wedding and the corpse at every funeral."

The Poppy Show Man

Basil Kong

Albert Calhoun was a heavy equipment operator who had a long career in road construction. He was never out of work as Jamaica had launched a program to upgrade the island's many unpaved roads. Each new road project usually lasted several years and took him to a different town.

When he was not working on the roadway, he was busy sewing his colorful outfits that earned him the nickname, "Poppy Show Man."

He would move into a town, buy a house, find a suitable female companion and set up house. Sometimes it would take a week to find a suitable partner, but it was never more than two weeks before he had sweet talked some woman to move in with him. He quickly became a part of the community, ate well, and enjoyed the comforts of a good home. He ended up fathering one or two children with each assignment.

Knowing these were temporary relationships, Albert ensured that his female companions had the wherewithal to support themselves and his children when he eventually moved on. He would give them the house he had bought and help them get jobs. One opened a grocery shop, one became a seamstress, another a hairdresser, while one ran a patty and ice-cream parlor.

Whenever Albert said goodbye to take on a new assignment, that was the last most of the women and children would see of him. In many cases, these women would marry someone else and his children got their 'broughtupsy' from their mother and stepfather.

After retiring from road building at sixty-five years of age, Albert became a tailor and soon became famous for his stylish and colorful clothes. He was never idle as customers came from far and near. He had already developed a reputation in every town he had lived for the outfits he wore as the poppy show man.

Millicent was his last child. Her mother was Betty, the woman who owned the grocery shop also had a bar and held Saturday night dances to support herself.

"Millicent, you cannot get married without inviting your father. It's unheard of," declared Betty.

"Mom, you know how much I love my dad, but when he walks me down the aisle, everybody will be looking at him. Is it too much to ask that on my wedding day, I should be the center of attention? My father has never been to a wedding where he was not the bride. And he has not been to a funeral where he was not the corpse. What am I going to do? Please help me out here. For once can't he just be Daddy at my wedding instead of the Poppy Show Man?"

"I will talk to him, Millicent, but I know he is hard at work sewing his outfit and gluing matching cloth onto his shoes. It's his daughter's wedding and he plans on putting on a spectacular show.

Sure enough, as soon as the organist started playing "Here comes the bride," all eyes were on the father, Mr. Albert Calhoun, otherwise known as the Poppy Show Man. He was decked out in canary yellow from head to toe. The yellow bolo hat was made from the same material as his suit, waistcoat, necktie, shoes and even his walking stick. Just as Millicent had predicted, he had stolen her big day.

His loving daughter, Millicent, dutifully grabbed his left elbow and tried hard to hold back tears as she walked down the aisle. She knew that no one was paying attention to her or would notice the beautiful white lace dress she was wearing because they were all staring at Poppy.

She heard the whispers, "What a way him look sharp? I have to get him to make me one of those suits."

"Did you notice that the sun went into hiding and covered itself with clouds when he came outta the car?"

"Me sorry for the daughter all the same, she no match for her handsome well-dressed father. And the poor husband must be intimidated. Him definitely not in the same league." "No man, him too tame." Everyone was craning their necks to get a glimpse of Poppy.

Vows were exchanged and then the Pastor gave the groom permission to kiss the bride.

The groom, Robert, whispered quickly in Millicent's ear," You're the most beautiful girl here. You will always be my shining star and I only have eyes for you." Those words made her realize that it didn't matter that Poppy had stolen her thunder. She had captured the prize by marrying the man she loved.

At the reception, both men and women crowded around Poppy to get a better look at his outfit. He was also a great dancer, so the ladies lined up to 'wheel and tun' with him. He had danced with every woman and girl pickney in attendance by the end of the night. The husbands seemed proud that Poppy was dancing with their wives.

In the corner of the dance floor, Millicent was wrapped in her husband's arms. Robert made her feel like she was the only person in the world and assured her that she would always be the center of his life. At that moment, Millicent did not care about the attention that Poppy was getting because she was with the man of her dreams.

Suddenly, the room got quiet, and all eyes were front and center. Poppy had taken the microphone to toast the happy couple.

"I rise to give the happy couple a toast." He reached into his pocket and pulled out two slices of toast and hand one to each of them. Everyone laughed and applauded.

"Well, all kidding aside, I am grateful you are all here sharing this proud moment with me. It is a privilege for me to give my beautiful daughter's hand in marriage to this fine young man. Robert, you are a lucky man. You have found a real treasure. I wish this awesome couple great happiness and I give them my blessings. Robert and Millicent, you make your father proud and I can't wait for my grandchildren."

There is a saying, "the only difference between a wedding and a funeral in Jamaica is that there is one less drunk at the funeral." Poppy never left the dance floor as even at seventy-seven years of age he had more stamina that most of the young boys there.

When his current lady love suggested that it was late and they should get ready to go, he objected and announced that not enough people had seen him yet.

When Poppy died at age 84 in Kingston, his then common-law wife, who knew his life story, made a great effort to inform all his previous lady companions and his biological children. The truth was that Millicent was one of six daughters and eight sons by six different women.

It was at his funeral that most of his children, whose ages ranged between 50 and 60, and his former lovers now in their 70s and 80s would meet each other for the first time.

He was laid out in an outfit that he himself had selected—a purple outfit from head to toe. While the viewing was only scheduled for four hours, they had to leave the casket open for two days as people crowded in to pay their respects and marvel at what he would be wearing to glory.

AUTHOR'S NOTE

Obeah is a system of spirituality and magic that was developed by enslaved Africans in Jamaica. Variations of it exist in other Caribbean islands under different names. It was practiced in secret having been outlawed. During slavery, it was a crime punishable by death if done by any 'Negro or other slave'. With the abolition of slavery, new laws were enacted with punishments that included flogging or imprisonment, among other penalties. The government of Jamaica recently abolished such colonial-era punishments, but the laws remain on the books. Religious leaders have opposed calls for decriminalization. In "Confessions of an Obeah Man," Moon Man Clay reveals some of his secrets and provides a look into the workings of the practice.

Confessions of an Obeah Man

Basil Kong

I come from a long line of Jamaican Obeah men. Almost everything I know was passed down from my father and grandfather. This knowledge goes all the way back to the days of slavery and Mother Africa.

My father once faked his own death and resurrection in an effort to increase his power over the people. In the heat of one of his impassioned sermons, he took a knife and cut his own throat. Several people ran when they saw the blood squirting. I kept everyone away from him. He laid on his back for effect and then started repeating: Kate a coy for a coy over and over until he stood up. Everyone was awestruck and regarded him as a dead man walking. Demand for his services skyrocketed as people were now captivated.

My parents named me Rufus Clay, sixty years ago, but people in my community call me "Moon Man Clay". They recognized long ago that like the moon, I can be bright and romantic on one side and dark, sometimes very dark on the other side.

Did you know that we belong to the Comfa or Wanga religion? The word Obeah is derived from the word 'Obeye' in the Twi dialect spoken by the Akan people in parts of Ghana. It means doing mysterious work.

People use obeah to harm or take revenge on their adversaries or to be empowered and to take control of their lives for personal success. Our ceremonies and sessions often end with the beating of drums and spirited dancing that culminates with frenzy and fainting. Our music has charms to soothe even the most savage beasts.

We are outlaws. Obeah was declared illegal in 1760 because the powers that be were fearful of the influence we had over the people. So much for freedom of religion. However, the law only served to publicize and increase the demand for our services. I can assure you that all those people who voted for the law consult Obeah men secretly. Many priests and parsons representing all religions, make their way across the island to access my services.

I was once arrested and found guilty in her majesty's court in Black River of taking money from a client under false pretenses. Before the judge sentenced me, I warned him that if he sent me to prison, bad things would happen to him. He replied: "You don't frighten me. I am sentencing you to twelve months in prison at hard labor." The next day, the guard at the prison told me that the judge had died of a heart attack. Sometimes I wish I didn't have to go to these lengths. Why won't people believe me? During my year in prison, all the guards brought me what I asked for including private visits from my girlfriends and live chickens for my rituals. They never denied a request. My fellow prisoners were equally accommodating and respectful. I did not find being in prison difficult. One of the other prisoners who was a ginnal or con man, from Kingston told everyone he met that I was a fraud. I told him that he would die at noon the next day and he suddenly fell ill and died that afternoon. I admit the timing was a little off.

The depth and extent of the superstition of Jamaicans is formidable. There is a fear of the veil of mystery surrounding obeah ceremonies. The irony is they all carry some of the secrets of the science that they learned as youths, and will believe, for as long as they live. While some will revere me, and do as I command, most fear me. The bravest of them tremble when they approach my temple and see eggshells, feathers, bones, teeth, chicken beaks, cemetery dirt, flags and stones, bay-rum, oils from all over the world and vinegar. There are bottles containing obeah mixtures and various herbs hanging from trees. This is where goats and fowls are sacrificed in mysterious blood rights and ceremonies. You enter at your own risk when you pass through my doors but make no mistake…the brave will be rewarded.

Once my father was summoned to the home of a rich lady who had been diagnosed with cancer and had only months to live. He asked for a live chicken. Everyone witnessed him sever the chicken's head and throw it into the crowd in the yard. He then demanded that it be brought back to him. When a brave soul returned it, my father reattached the head to the chicken and promised that as long as the chicken lived, the rich lady would also live. This lady's helpers took excellent care of that chicken and she rewarded him handsomely. Unfortunately, the chicken was killed and eaten by a mongoose two years later. As predicted, the lady died soon after that. They should have taken better care of the chicken.

My father added a new wrinkle in 1935 when he adopted the teachings of Lauron William de Laurence, an American who sold books and goods dealing with the occult and magic by mail. Although the Jamaica government banned all de Laurence books, my father had easy access to them. My great-great-grandfather worked on the plantation owned by the infamous Annie Palmer, the White Witch of Rose Hall near Montego Bay. He helped her bury the bodies of three husbands under the house. Annie's last husband killed her along with my great-great-grandfather. It was rumored that they were secret lovers.

My father commanded that no one should discipline me in any way and instead encouraged the devil to play an even greater role in my life. I was never beaten as a child. When other children were beaten and ordered to cease their undesirable behavior, I was encouraged to be even worse. While all the other pickney dem were punished for the bad things they did, I was always proud to tell me puppa all the wicked things I did, and he was very proud of me. He delighted in my escapades. He would say: "Son, you are not nearly bad enough. Use your imagination. You can do better than that."

When I am not wearing my colorful red robe and cap, I look like everyone else. I may seem like just another man because my black heart is hidden from your view. You may approach me, innocently, not knowing the risk you take. If you offend me in any way, I can bring down sorrow, distress, injury, and calamity on you. All I need is just a hair from your head, a discarded fingernail or a toenail. I can bestow a curse on anyone with or without their knowledge. Like a devil in street clothes, if you pass or brush up against me, a chill will come over you, or a puff of wind blow across your face. I use strong medicine.

One of the oldest secret society is Christianity. After Jesus was crucified, his disciples organized secret meetings in the catacombs. They celebrated communion by symbolically eating the flesh and drinking the blood of Jesus. When word got around, they were accused of being cannibals. When they rescued abandoned babies,

Christians were rumored to be eating them. That gave the Roman authorities an excuse to hunt and kill them.

Do you consider what I do evil? Organized religion has been man's main excuse for inflicting evil. If you really want to be a witness, just think of the evil deeds that have been done by Christians. The Crusaders went around the world asking people if they believed in Jesus. If the response was no, they killed them immediately. The Spanish inquisition exterminated some three million people. Under orders from the Catholic Pope, thousands of Huguenots were killed in 1572. In the eighteenth century, thousands of Protestants were killed, including women with infants sucking at their mother's breasts in the very church where they were worshiping. To me that was evil.

In the old days, Catholic priests would go to the deathbed of a church member and guarantee his ascension into heaven if he left his house and land to the church when he died. When the poor parishioner passed on, the church would claim the property and throw the wife of the deceased and children out to become homeless.

Throughout the centuries, priests have raped little boys and girls in the sanctuary of the church. One day, I plan to create an "Anti-Christ Museum" in Jamaica to depict and document the horrendous atrocities these 'moral monsters' have done in the name of 'Jesus'.

Everywhere the English conquered they brought missionaries and Bibles. In a very short time, they had exchanged bibles for land. They enriched themselves and enslaved the people. They taught Black people that everything foreign was good and that they should replace their thoughts with English ideas. They did such a good job brainwashing to the people we may never be able to liberate our minds from mental slavery. The wrongs done to the people of Jamaica have never been righted.

In Jamaica, we celebrate excesses, both good and bad. We may be the greatest athletes, poets, scholars, and musicians in the world, but on the other hand, we can be the most heartless criminals as well. I believe many Jamaicans do not think through things before they act. Some are thoughtless. An angry man will come to me and put in an order: "I just want him dead." This is typically in response to finding out that someone has stolen money from him, disrespected him or had an affair with his wife. Why hurt the man who gave you a job? When his business fails you will have no job. Or why hurt your doctor who treats your family. People don't consider that their intended victim has relatives who will retaliate. It's like a man who poured gasoline in his water tank to kill mosquitoes and only to realize he had now had no drinking water.

We like quick fixes. People are obsessed with magic and miracles. Popular culture in Jamaica nurtures the popularity of Obeah because of our obsession with style over substance, manipulation over honest dealing and most importantly, selfishness and 'bad mind'. We overlook evil in our community and criticize what our neighbors wear. I pray for the day when we can all live like brothers and sisters. Well, let me take that back because the worst fights I have seen are between siblings over their inheritance at their father's grave. We are only human and human nature is weak. Can a dog not bark, and can birds stop singing?

I do not consider anything I do evil. I am well rewarded for my services. When pretty women come to me, they willingly offer themselves and we both enjoy our time together. They know my power and want me on their side.

I can fix games. Before a cricket match, I set strong obeah by killing a chicken at each stump on the cricket pitch and draining the blood around the wickets while reciting a secret incantation that guarantees victory for the home team.

Sickness, death, disappearances and mysterious happening follow in my wake. The use of knives and guns are for impatient amateurs. My 'science' is much more powerful. Once you gaze into my evil eyeballs, you are at my mercy. It is so much better to be my client and seek my protection from evil forces. If you choose not to retain me, you will likely become my next victim wondering why calamity has suddenly befallen you. Some people call their misfortune "bad luck".

I am the proverbial "Dr. Jekyll and Mr. Hyde". Two extremely different personalities in the same body. I switch between evil and good frequently. To children and all who seek my assistance for any number of problems, I am kind, generous, extremely polite and engaging. To anyone who wishes to harm me or anyone I have been engaged to harm, I am ruthless and brutal.

Good and evil is present in all of us. I know a man who has killed several people in the most horrific ways but could never refuse an old woman who needs help. He gives a lot of money to the church and is loving and kind to his family and friends. Is he evil or good? What is the formula for determining who is bad and who is good? Should you judge a person by the worse thing they did? How about the best thing they did? If you found out that Mother Teresa once had an abortion, would that change how you felt about her life of good deeds. That is what usually happens. Is a man a liar if he tells one lie or lies all the time?

I live and work in the shadows of Jamaican society. I am openly venerated but secretly feared and believed. Most people are embarrassed to be associated with us and shrug off what we do as nonsense and superstition. They deny subscribing to Obeah and overtly practice Christianity, but if you scratch the surface, they are uncomfortable and even tremble at the mention of the word "Obeah".

If a student knows that his mother has been to me to assure that he will pass his exam, he will be more confident and increase his likelihood of a pass. But sometimes a boy will not study believing that Obeah will assure him a pass. Obeah only helps those who help themselves.

Obeah will be part of the Jamaican landscape forever. We are too insecure. They come to me to feel empowered. We are also too invested in short cuts. Our propensity for taking short cuts contributes to failure. Instead of working hard, we look for the quick and easy way. I advise my clients to make themselves lovable if they want to be loved; be loyal employees and friends and that there is no substitute for hard work. While I may give our Olympic champions a little help, they would never be the great champions without sweat, sacrifice and tears.

I am the best Obeah man in Jamaica because I learned from the best. I consult with fellow members of my craft, read constantly about my craft, and always follow up with my clients to learn from their experience so I can be more effective.

I am a threat to everybody because, if I merely tell someone that something bad is going to happen to them, that is all that is required to spoil their day as they obsess until they decide to pay me to remove the curse. Then they get relief. What a cheap price to pay for peace of mind. If they return to tell me that they still feel anxious or I didn't achieve their objectives, I tell them that they didn't pay me enough. They will pay a lot for relief from my curse.

I prescribe various ointments with descriptive names: "Duppy conqueror" for those who are afraid of being haunted by duppy;

"Isle of Fire" for revenge; frankincense and myrrh for depression; "compelling oil" to make your children and others obedient; "oil make you stay here" for those who want to keep their loved ones from leaving them; "commanding oil" to control the person; "love oil" to compel a member of the opposite sex to love them.

There is no loyalty among our clan. Our loyalty is to our clients and of course to ourselves. George is one of my Obeah brethren who was a real snake. He was blamed for every strange and mysterious thing that happened in his community. Whenever dogs, cats and goats went missing, everyone looked at him. When they heard strange noises after dark, someone was bound to say "George is up to no good again." His wife was often the victim of his dark side. Each time he had a confrontation with her, screams and yelling could be heard deep into the night along with his daily promises to her: "When I die, I will dig my way up and out of the grave to come back and haunt you for the rest of your life!"

She feared him and came to me for help. Well, after the wife hired me, George died abruptly under strange and mysterious circumstances. With my advice, the funeral had a closed casket. After the burial, the wife drank white rum and celebrated as if there was no tomorrow. Her cheerfulness attracted the attention of her neighbors who asked her why she wasn't afraid. "Your husband knew the 'science' and told you that when he died, he would dig his way up and out of the grave and haunt you for the rest of your life." She put down her drink hard on the kitchen table and said, "Let the rass man dig. I had him buried upside down." With my help, George is digging his way to hell.

I bring religion, prayer, faith, and western medicine together under one roof. Spirituality and medicine belong together as together they become the cornerstone of health and wellbeing. Sickness and sin have many physicians. All human beings have fears, and everyone is a candidate for the Obeah treatment that can banish anxiety from daily living.

Has your spiritual growth stopped? Obeah can help. Are you afraid that your lover is planning to leave you? Obeah can help. Are you being haunted by duppy? Obeah can help. Are you depressed? Obeah can help. Are you in pain for no known cause? Obeah can help. Become a happy, cheerful person, see your Obeah man today and be astonished! With the help of your local obeahman, you too, can be happy and healthy again.

We have no shortage of customers, patrons, clients, or patients so here is some free advice:

1. If you are lonely, light a candle, hit a drum, or knock on a table with a spoon thirteen times, close your eyes and listen over and over to the drum or the knocks on the table when you are not knocking the table.

2. If you are haunted by duppy, walk exactly one mile backwards. If you are walking backwards, duppy cannot follow you.

3. If you have lost someone close to you by death, migration or separation, boil some 'single bible' and take a bath in it. While you are in the bath, recite twelve times: "Deliver I from loneliness. Deliver I from pain. Let my loved one come home again."

You can be happy and well again. We are a wonderful supplement to whatever help is being provided by your medical doctor, minister, or therapist. Obeah can free you from your fears, anxieties, bitterness, anger, and fill your heart with gladness. If you are unconvinced and unconverted to Obeah, discuss it with your fearless and heroic Obeah man as soon as possible. "Try it nuh?" Become a happier, cheerful person. See your local Obeah man today and be astonished! With the help of your local obeah-man, you too, can be happy and healthy again.

AUTHOR'S NOTE

Although Jamaica is a small island there has always been a gulf between city life and country life. There is a stigma with being a "country bwoy" and the many jokes highlighting the naiveté of country folk. When visiting the city, you are warned to beware people who might try to sell you a public park as farmland. People move to the city for greater access to many benefits such as education, jobs, culture, and healthcare. While many succeed, some face social alienation with the loss of community and access to nature. Brother Maxie never quite adjusted to city life and was never happy until he went back to "country."

The Resurrection of
Brother Maxie

Basil Kong

In the 1950's, people who lived in Woodside District believed they lived in the healthiest and happiest place on earth. The community was blessed with cool breezes and daily sunshine that kept their personalities warm. Frequent rains provided fresh clean water that was stored in drums outdoors, and inside the houses in Panay Jars with a brimstone on the bottom to keep it cool and refreshing. The pristine green landscape and resulting air quality commonly associated with health and optimism kept their lungs clean and their thinking straight.

They were proud of their homegrown food. Each household had their own plot of ground producing corn, peas, yams, cassava, sweet potatoes, dashine, pumpkins, bananas that they ate green or ripe and cocoa. Some had their own cows, chickens, and hogs. Everyone had their own "cho-cho" arbor because babies and children love to eat it. Crops were planted according to the calendar in MacDonald's Farmers Almanac. There was no need to buy too much from the shop except for some oil, bread, rice, salt, and salt-fish. Someone in the District made oil from coconuts and wet sugar from sugarcane. Oranges, grapefruit, and other citrus fruit was abundant. Someone cut a hundred limbs from trees and stuck them into the ground as fence posts and it soon became a line of trees. It is that easy to grow things. People lived long because life was good, and they were kind to each other. They believed that if you were honest, sober, industrious, and considerate of others success in life would be assured.

On Saturday nights, the Herbie Arnold Rumba Band would provide a little entertainment and gave them a chance to "wind up their waists" and "liven up themselves." On Sunday, they worshipped the Lord and thanked Him for his blessings. Everyone enjoyed praying together and making a joyful noise. Although some wished Bra Bone would not sing so loud because there was nothing joyful about his voice and he tended to drown out everybody else.

The story of Brother Maxie was well known in the district. When he was a boy his mother found herself in desperate straits and could no longer feed and clothe him. She appealed to a Chinese family who were shopkeepers. Old Mr. Chen and Ms. Ada already had two sons Harry and Charles who were about the same age and so they agreed to raise him as their own. The boys got along just fine.

Old Chen arranged for all three boys to attend high school in Kingston. Although his fellow students were mean to him when they realized he was a country bumpkin, Brother Maxie did not let it bother him. He just kept his head down and graduated eventually becoming an engineer. He was never without work as employers preferred to hire people from St. Elizabeth because of their reputation for honesty and hard work. "When you say you are from St. Elizabeth, that's all the recommendation you need."

He was making good money and saving most of it as he lived in a tenement yard where he shared kitchen and bathrooms with several other people. Although many women tried to befriend him, he never found the right one and continued living as a bachelor.

When he was thirty-three years old, he suddenly became sick and was admitted to Kingston Public Hospital. He explained to the doctors that he felt lifeless, tired, depressed, had no appetite and was losing a lot of weight. The doctors prescribed some pills, but they did not help.

He tried going to church but never felt comfortable as he found the Kingstonians too hypocritical for his liking. Many could dress up nice for church, but their lives were devoid of honesty, integrity, sympathy or caring for others. He was suspicious of people as he had been betrayed by several people he thought he could trust. He could never be sure that someone was not trying to steal and take advantage of him. He became even more sullen.

He became so sick that he thought he was going to die. He stayed awake at night worrying about threats on his life by gangs. People whispered: "The man was sick, sick, sick, sick, sick."

Believing that he was terminally ill, he packed up his troubles and his clothes and headed back to Woodside. Like an old elephant, he thought he was going back to where he was born to die.

By the time he returned, his adopted Chinese family had closed the shop and migrated to Canada, so he moved into the living quarters and reclaimed the shop. The neighbors took turns visiting him, bringing their plates of curry goat and rice, pumpkin soup with corn meal dumplings, roast yam, callaloo and salt-fish, brown stew chicken, June plum juice, custard apple and soursop juice and best of all, corn pone and sweet potato pudding. The carrot juice with sweet milk and dragon stout hit the spot and brought a smile to his face and lead back in his pencil. He even developed a strong liking for "flumbadip" that they made from salt mackerel and coconut custard with red annatto.

The minister from the Moravian Church heard he was back and visited him accompanied by the choir. They sang songs of praise, laid hands on him and took turns praying. Soon he no longer felt poorly and was well enough to visit the neighbors, (no appointment necessary) sit a spell and enjoy a conversation. He delighted in walking and talking with whoever was available. And they all showered him with lots of broad smiles, hugs, and kisses. In three months, his appetite returned and he was sleeping like a baby.

Miss Dorothy was a good cook and a charming country girl who attended to his every need. Maybe there is something to food being the way to a man's heart as her specialty was the "flumbadip" he craved. As a member of the church choir, she sang his favorite hymns. They took long walks holding hands on their frequent visits to friends and neighbors. They had fallen in love and he asked her to marry him.

Miss Dorothy looked absolutely radiant as she walked down the aisle on her wedding day. The entire community came out for the big day and everyone was invited to the grand reception at the social center adjoining the church. Their union bore two beautiful girls that they named Izet and Sylvie as well as a son that they named Francisco. Brother Maxie now had everything to live for.

The money he was planning to use for his funeral expenses was enough to buy the car he needed to make trips to Kingston as well as to the doctor and dentist. He also used it to serve the community, if anyone had to go to the hospital or a student needed to return to school, he was ready to transport them.

He planted carrot seeds in the soil behind the house and reopened the shop, which soon became a popular place to enjoy a beer, some lemonade, a bulla, or a piece of bread and butter. He even offered homemade patties and fried chicken. People would gather around, play dominoes and dance to the music from his Telefunken radio. They especially like to listen to cricket from JBC. He attended church regularly and even taught a Sunday School class.

Whenever he traveled to Kingston to buy supplies, he would visit his friends at the tenement yard who were surprised at how robust and healthy he looked as they remembered him as a dejected skeleton. He extolled the virtues of country life and convinced his old friend John to join him in Woodside.

Bother Maxie and Miss Dorothy enjoyed ten years of wedded bliss, but it was not to last. His sweet, attentive wife died in childbirth along with their fourth child. He could not be consoled. He became reclusive and no longer desired the company of anyone and found that the only thing that dulled the pain was devil rum which he drank every day. He made up a mournful song that he sang whenever he got drunk.

> When I die, don't you bury me at all
> Just lay my bones in alcohol
> One bottle of beer to my head and one to my feet
> and let the world find out that my bones can be cured.

The neighbors would shake their heads in pity and the children tried to help but he was just not up to doing anything useful. His oldest daughter Sylvia became a nurse and migrated to the United States and did well for herself. In fact, she was able to sponsor her brother and sister. Although reluctant at first, Brother Maxie finally gave in and migrated too. However, after three months he was desperate to get back to Jamaica. He ended up returning to Woodside where he lived on the remittance money his children sent each month.

Brother Maxie had his difficulties, but he is the father of three successful children. One year they brought three of his grandchildren home to visit him. They took him to Sandals, an all-inclusive hotel in Montego Bay for a week where he ate to his heart's content, enjoyed the nightly entertainment and was happy drinking as much liquor as he wanted. He thought he was in heaven. He even sat down to have a drink at the bar with a visitor from the United States, who introduced himself as Joe from Arkansas. With great pride he introduced Joe to his family, and they ended up discussing his drinking habit. Joe asked him why he was trying to kill himself when he has these beautiful grandchildren to live for. Brother Maxie put his drink down and said: "Sir, ever so often someone says something that changes the direction of a life. You have changed mine. I will never again have another drink of rum. Children deserve to know their grandfather."

He shook hands with Joe and walked jauntily down the beach to play with his grandchildren.

Acknowledgements

We are grateful to those who gave us a drink of water when we were thirsty, a bulla when we were hungry, and advice and inspiration when needed. They are too numerous to mention, and many names have been forgotten but Miss Pukus, Bra Bone, Mass Polite, Little man, Miss Agnes, Keri, Mrs. Welds, Miss Byfield, Mrs. Betton, Mr. Bennett, Dennis, Ivy, Beverly, Sonia, Monty, Newton, Bunny, Steve, Molly, Teddy, Rosie, Pepsi, Dudo, Bredda, Cigar, Beth, Dawn, Pauline, Hopkin, Bob, Brian, Lloydie, Joyce, Rev. Cadogan, June, Mary, , Aunt Joe, Ms. Erma, Ms. Aggie, Ms. Rachael, Sadam, Captain Mills and Rev. Craig and Punkus come to mind.

We are also deeply indebted to the people who inspired the stories in this book. Many thanks to Marcia Guthrie who shared some of her experiences that contributed to the "Bed and Breakfast Blues" story; to the actor and playwright Debra Ehrhardt for her insights and suggestions; to Carole Little and Toni Laman for reading and editing the manuscript, and to Pat Bignall and Earl Adams who helped with photographs. And special thanks to Lena Rose, of Minna Press publishing, whose enthusiasm and work on this project was remarkable.

About the Authors

Basil Kong attended Simpson College on a track scholarship setting a record in the 400 meters. He would go on to earn master's and doctorate degrees in Guidance and Counselling, and Educational Psychology, respectively. He later pursued a law degree and is a member of the Georgia Bar.

Kong retired at age 65 after serving 20 years as the CEO of the Association of Black Cardiologists. He returned to live in Jamaica where he researched and wrote the book *Bad Boy from Jamaica*. He now lives in rural Georgia with his wife of 36 years, Stephanie, who is president and CEO of Zoe Pediatrics. They have four children and six grandchildren. Kong writes a weekly column for the *Upson County Beacon*.

Glen Laman attended college on academic scholarships graduating with bachelor and master's degrees in Biology and Business Administration, respectively. He had an exciting career in IT as a programmer and project manager working for several Fortune 500 companies. At age 60, Laman pursued a doctorate in business administration and published his research in the highly acclaimed book, *Jamaican Entrepreneurship*. He lives in Florida with his wife Toni, who is a retired science teacher. They have two children and three grandchildren.

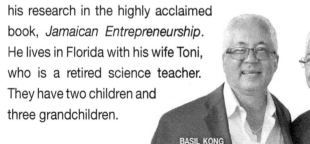

BASIL KONG

GLEN LAMAN

CPSIA information can be obtained
at www.ICGtesting.com
Printed in the USA
BVHW080756261021
619846BV00005B/253